I0610029

W. P. Frank Cabler

Don't Go to Hell

W. P. Frank Cabler

Don't Go to Hell

ISBN/EAN: 9783337392673

Printed in Europe, USA, Canada, Australia, Japan

Cover: Foto ©Andreas Hilbeck / pixelio.de

More available books at **www.hansebooks.com**

DON'T GO TO HELL.

LECTURES AND SERMONS

——BY——

W. P. FRANK CABLER.

PADUCAH, KY.
DILDAY & VAN SENDEN.
1894.

PREFACE.

If you find a single flower on the pages of this book, store it in the closet of your memory, so that its aroma may not be wasted. If by reading this book a single sinner finds Christ, or a single Christian finds consolation, the author will be paid for his trouble.

AUTHOR.

SURROUNDING CIRCUMSTANCES.

I got my early education on a farm, a'hold of the plow handles, behind a mule from sun-up to sun-down. A mule don't learn a man much about books; but he learns him a good deal of mule sense. I would a great deal rather have good old practical mule sense without a good education than to have a good education without practical mule sense. When I talk to a crowd I want the people to understand me. I don't care what kind of a hammer I use to hit the nail on the head, just so I drive it in. I once heard an educated fool make a talk. He picked every big word out of the dictionary and when he got through nobody knew what he was talking about. When I say "pisen" everybody in this crowd knows what I mean. You know that I mean something that will kill. I could say poison, but sometimes "pisen" suits me better. I don't care how good your education is, you will understand me, but if you havn't got any education you'll understand me, too.

You have all got hearts and brains and souls, whether you have got education or not, and it is the heart, and brain and soul that I want to touch, and not the education. If you want to learn anything about grammar you had better go home and start to school, for you ain't going to learn anything about it here; neither am I going to attempt to learn you much about the Bible, for the meanest and most ignorant 'man in this house has got Bible sense enough to know that he is going straight down the road to Hell, and he has also got Bible sense enough to know how to turn around and go back towards Heaven. I just want to pile up your sins before you and block your pathway to Hell. I want to give the Devil a little pisen, and if you find it hard medicine to take now, you will find after it has had its effect that you'll feel much better. The doctor never thinks about how bitter his medicine is, it's the result he's after.

Some of you may think that I am a'going to talk to broadcloth and Satan, but I ain't. Neither am I a'going to talk to calico and Jehu's. I am talking to people and not to wealth. I don't care how rich you are. Your riches will buy you a carriage and a mansion here on earth, but it won't save your soul. A man can take one dollar and buy a ticket straight to Hell, but he couldn't bribe God to let him one inch nearer

Heaven with all of the millions of all of the millionaires of earth. The Devil thinks a heap of money. He'll lie for it; he'll steal for it; he'll gamble for it, and the meanest of all, he'll ruin men's souls, make orphans and widows and then starve them to death by selling whisky for it.

You ain't too poor to be good, and you ain't too rich to be good. So many people say, "I'd be a better man or a better woman if it wasn't for surrounding circumstances." Hell's full of people that had surrounding circumstances. If you plant corn and let the weeds grow and don't plow it and then sit down and say you are afraid that you'll not make any corn on account of surrounding circumstances. Surrounding circumstances will starve you to death if you depend on that corn, but if you get up and hoe out them weeds and plow the corn you will make surrounding circumstances agreeable to the growing of corn, and you will have a crop and be all right. If you can't be good in your surrounding circumstances get up and make surrounding circumstances so that you can be good.

If I step on your pet corn don't snap back like a yellow cur dog, but do something and get rid of your corn so it can't be stepped on any more. Out in Colorado during a time when mining excitement was at fever heat, I was standing in a gambling house. Oh, yes; I've been in gambling houses, and almost everywhere else on earth. You see, I've devoted fifteen years of my life to continual travel, and lost my last dollar many a time at faro or poker. In the early days of Leadville the gambling houses were crowded every night in the week, Sunday night included. Miners, prospectors, tourists, rich and poor were all alike trying their fortunes at one or the other of the various games. The proprietors, with an eye to business, saw that whisky flowed as free as water, so that the suckers would bite more rapidly. Old gray-haired men that were probably pillows of the Church back in some eastern or southern home, while in their homes would not even think of going to a gambling house, out in Leadville among strangers would forget God and wife and children, and in the evening take in the town and finally drop into a gambling house just to look on. They would make surrounding circumstances so that the temptation would be too strong to resist, and just for fun they would purchase a few chips, and from that moment on the Devil would take possession of their souls. If they won they would be sure to return the next night to add to their ill-gotten gains. If they lost they would be sure to return just to get even. So night after night the same old faces could be seen, sometimes beaming with hope and other times frowning with rage, and when the last shining dollar had left the pocket, lost in despair.

The Devil is fishing with poles and lines and hooks all over this earth, and every hook is baited with a big fat worm of deceit, and the sucker that nibbles now and gets a taste is sure to bite after a while and get the hook hung in his gills so that the Devil can easily land him in Hell. The shrewd fish will keep away from the Devil's baited hooks. Keep out of evil company. Keep out of the saloons and gambling hells and other places where vice is bred. Ice will make things cold, and fire will make things hot. If you don't want to catch the small-pox, keep away from it. If you don't want to be a drunkard, keep away from whisky. If you don't want to raise your sons up to be gamblers, keep cards out of your house and keep your children out of other houses where they have cards.

Let surrounding circumstances be agreeable to vice, and you'll have vice. Let surrounding circumstances be agreeable to Christianity, and you'll have Christianity. You can't plant corn and raise potatoes, and you can't raise much of either if you don't keep them out of bad company by cultivating them and keeping the weeds away.

I stood in one of the large gambling houses of Leadville. I had just got up from the faro table with three hundred and seventy-five dollars ahead of the game. A young man walked up to me and remarked that I was very lucky, and said he had never gambled in his life, but that he felt tempted to-night to try his luck, as he was badly in need of money. He had been going to that place every night for over two weeks, just as a looker-on, but the temptation was never strong enough to make him play until he saw me win as much as I did, he took five dollars out of his pocket in a kind of a nervous way and walked over to the faro bank and invested it in chips, sat down and began playing. I felt a little interested so I walked over to see how the tenderfoot would play. At first things appeared to be running his way, but soon his luck changed and he had to go down in his pocket for another five. He kept playing until he had lost fifty dollars on the layout, then he raised up from his chair, reached down in his pockets and pulled out four silver dollars, the perspiration was standing in great beads on his forehead and he was trembling all over with nervous excitement. He threw the four dollars down on the high card open, then pulled a pistol

from his pocket and said: The fifty dollars I
have just lost was for my poor old widowed
mother and little fatherless brothers and sisters;
I went to the express office this evening to send
it to her but the office was closed, so I had to
wait until morning; but now I have lost it and
she is sick and poor and will starve if she can't get
help. The four dollars I have on that card is
the last cent I have on earth, if I loose it I will
blow out my brains.

The cold and heartless dealer simply smiled
as he pulled out the top card, four of clubs was
up; chances were in favor of the young man
who was then standing with the muzzle of the
pistol against his own temple. I found myself
growing desperate. I, like many others, knew
that if anyone attempted to take the pistol away
from him he would pull the trigger and end his
life. Just as the dealer was about to pull the
four of clubs out of the box a happy thought
struck me. I had three hundred and seventy-
five dollars in my pocket that I had just won. I
needed the money but I felt that I could afford
to loose it to save a son for a mother. "Hold,"
I cried to the dealer, "just one minute; if the
young man looses I will loan him twice the
amount he was going to send his mother if he
will promise never to gamble again; he can pay
it back if he chooses, when he gets able."

The card was drawn, the two of spades was up, the high card had lost. I shoved a hundred dollar bill across the table, the young man lowered the pistol and took the bill with tears of honest gratitude streaming down both cheeks. After taking down my name and address he held his hand towards high heaven and swore by all he held sacred that he would never enter another gambling house or gamble so long as he lived. As the young man walked out the dealer looked up at me and remarked that I was the biggest sucker in the west. Old acquaintances made fun of me and said the fellow never intended to kill himself and would probably try the same game somewhere else in less than a week. But I could not help feeling that I had seen the determination to die in that young man's eyes.

Two years had passed and I had almost forgot the affair, when I received a draft for two hundred dollars and a letter from the young man. He said that after leaving the gambling house that night he immediately went to his boarding house and went to bed with the prayer his mother taught him in his early childhood ringing in his mind. He got up the next morning and sent his mother seventy-five dollars. The remaining twenty-five he soon spent in looking for something to do. When the last dollar had left his pocket he got a position at small wages, but now he was in a prosperous condition and was able to pay me back the money I had loaned him. He begged me to take the other hundred as a present, if I needed it; if not, to give it to some unfortunate, miserable wretch and let the great good I had done for him be doubled. I also received a letter from his old mother. When he sent me the money he told her the story. Every line and every word of her letter was permeated with gratitude. She thanked me over and over again for what I had done for her boy, the sole dependence of her declining years. She told me that her son had professed religion and was a good Christian. I was urgently invited to visit the family.

A few months afterward I happened to be within fifteen miles of the town they lived in. I had the time so I concluded to run over and see them. What a picture of domestic comfort and happiness I saw, and if I had been a long lost son and brother they could not have treated me better. The old gray-haired mother told me that a day never passed without her praying to God for me. Her son has never played a card or gambled a cent since that almost fatal night. Two weeks visits to the gambling rooms came very near wrecking this now happy and prosperous family; came very near burying a loving son and surrounding a mother and three little orphan children in sorrow and poverty.

I, myself, have never gambled a cent, played at cards, or knowingly entered a place where gambling was carried on since I saw that old grateful mother and loving children whose happiness the money I won came near destroying by encouraging the son and brother to his first and last gambling.

The circumstances surrounding the young man that went to the gambling house just to look on were made by himself. He knew right from wrong; he placed himself in a position to be tempted and fell almost to the point of committing suicide. The night he left that gambling house he determined to keep away from all evil influences. He is now a Christian gentleman, happy and prosperous.

While surrounding circumstances have a great deal to do with people's lives, people have a great deal to do with surrounding circumstances. The man who will keep out of the reach of snakes is not likely to die with snake bites. The man that will walk all over rattlesnakes may not get bit, but ninety-nine times out of a hundred he will. It won't do to trust snakes and it won't do to trust whisky, and it won't do to trust any kind of evil. Let four good boys run with one bad boy and nine chances to one, it won't be long before the result will be five bad boys, and so it is with men. I have heard of one bad woman wrecking the morals of a whole town. She was beautiful, educated, and apparently fitted to be a leader in society, but her heart was as black as sin itself. Her home was one of fashion; the young girls and boys swarmed around her; she was the great social center; no social gathering was complete without her; the ball room and theatre she idolized. Christian parents ignored her love for dance and the opera and encouraged their daughters in seeking her society on account of her polished society ways. The commencement of wholesale ruin was in the parlors of her fashionable home. Lemonade clashed with wine, then wine without the lemonade, then champagne and further on beer and whiskey, until innocent girls and careless boys had lost reason and become drunk with liquor and passion. Virtue lost its price in nightly revelries. Many once pure girls hung their heads in shame, thousands of tears were shed by many poor mothers and fathers tottering on towards the grave with broken hearts, looking back at drunken sons and fallen daughters. I tell you fifteen years of travel from place to place and knocking up against the cold sides of this world has taught me that but few are able to withstand temptation. One snake in the Garden of Eden caused the fall of the human race. Encourage one snake in the Eden of home or sur-

roundings and he will pluck the fruit from the
tree of knowledge and offer it in so many tempting ways that innocent girls and noble boys will
hardly be able to resist, and once down, it's
mighty hard to get up.   Any true Christian is
ever ready to lend a helping hand to the fallen,
but there are so many people in the world that
are not true Christians, and many of them when
they come across some fallen wretch will give
him a kick and send him further on his down-
ward career.   I for one have a greater admira-
tion for a Salvation Army going along the streets
shaking tambourines and beating drums and
reaching down in gutters of iniquity and taking
by the hand the nameless, the poor and the
ragged and offering up prayers to God for their
repentence, than I have for the man or woman
going by in broadcloth or satin and treating with
silent contempt the fallen neighbor.   Ashamed
to do good on the streets and only willing to
work for Christ while standing on Brussels carpet in some fashionable church and listening to
the tune of a ten thousand dollar organ.

The Jews plead for the crucifixion of our
Savior, who tramped from place to place, poor
and travel-stained without a place to lay his
head.   And I tell you if Christ would come back
now and live as he did then, there are plenty of
fashionable church members that are not Jews

that would repeat the crucifixion if they could, but if Christ would return, living in a mansion, riding in a carriage and dressed in broadcloth, they would grab him by the hand and say how do you Christ, I'm glad to meet you.

There is just as much religion in a base drum as a ten thousand dollar organ. It's the way you beat it; it's the way you play it. There is just as much religion in rags and jeans as broadcloth and satin. God don't care anything about your drum or your organ, your rags or your fine clothes; it's your earnestness—your soul. The fellow that hollers the loudest against the doctor when he's well, will call the most for the doctor when he is sick. There are thousands of people that while in good health go on day after day, committing sin after sin, careless of the laws of God, but when they fall in sickness, tortured with pain, looking at death staring them in the face, they will then think of God and Heaven and Hell, and with a loud voice wrung from the very heart, of fear, call on the God whom they had so often ignored. Bob Ingersoll says according to the religion of Jesus Christ the wicked believer may commit all of the crimes in the annals of history, but if between the last breath and death he calls on God he goes to Heaven, and a good disbeliever that leads an honest, moral, truthful life simply because he

don't call on God goes to Hell. In order to show
you where Ingersoll is wrong, I will quote one of
his illustrations. He said a farmer that was
honest and moral and just, but disbelieved the
Bible, died, and his soul was immediately wafted
up to the Golden Gates of Heaven. St. Peter
met it and said, "Where are you from?." "I'm
from the earth." "What was your business?"
"I was a farmer." "What kind of a life did you
lead?" "I lead an honest and moral life and
took good care of my family." Did you pay
your debts?" "Yes, and left enough money behind to pay my funeral expenses." Did you
believe in the Bible?" "No." "What, didn't
believe in the snake story and the rib story and
the whale and Jonah story?" "No." "Didn't
you call on God before you died?" "No."
"Send him to Hell."

Next brother soul from the earth appeared before St. Peter. "Where are you from?" "I'm
from the earth." What was your business?"
"I was cashier in the First National Bank in the
city of Chicago." "Did you ever steal anything?" "I don't like to talk about myself."
"But you must." "Did you ever steal anything?" "I run away with two hundred and
fifty thousand dollars belonging to the bank."
"Did you take anything else with you?" "Yes,
I took my neighbor's wife." "Did you leave

any money behind to take care of your wife and children?" "No, my confidence was so great in God I thought he would take care of them." "You believed in the Bible then." "Oh yes." "Did you believe in the rib story and snake story and other miracles of the Bible?" "Yes, I believed in all the miracles of the Bible, and always wished that there were more, so that I could show God what confidence I had in him." "Give him a harp; let the band play."

That is Ingersoll's version. Mine is different. Ingersol says the honest, moral, truthful, disbelieving farmer was a good man. I deny it. One must be something more than honest, moral and truthful to be good. One must be obedient. You have got a boy. You say, "Johnnie, here is a dime, run over to the store and get me a dime's worth of salt." And Johnnie starts and in half an hour you go out in the yard and find him playing marbles. You say, "Johnnie, I told you to go and get me some salt; go immediately," and you go back in the house and Johnnie goes off with a crowd of boys to play baseball. What do you think of that boy? It's not mean to play marbles; it's not mean to play baseball, but it's mean to disobey the parent, and the next time you catch Johnnie you give him a licking for his disobedience. Ingersoll's farmer was honest and just, truthful and moral,

but he was disobedient. He refused to obey a
very important commandment of God, he refused
to carry the cross of Christ, and for his disobedience he gets Hell. Ingersoll's bank cashier
believed in the Bible, but while in health cared
nothing for its teachings, and went on day after
day piling sin on sin, but finally when he saw
that he could sin no more, that he had to die,
between the last breath and death he called on
God, and Ingersoll says his soul was immediately
wafted up through the Golden Gates of Heaven
to hear the band play for ever more. That I
deny. While the Bible teaches us that the
eleventh hour is all right, if we do truly repent.
But do the people that go through life believing
in God, and yet refusing to obey his commandments, apparently waiting for the last moment
to rectify the sins of an entire lifetime, truly repent. I say no, not one time out of a hundred.
After they have committed so many sins and
finally fall on a bed of disease and see death
staring them coldly in the face, they look back
in the dim distance and see the Devil with
a pitch fork loaded with burning brimstone, and
they smell the fumes of Hell and get scared.
They look in front and hear divine music floating out from the golden harps of Heaven's happy
Angels, and they want Heaven. There is no
repentence about it, they simply want Heaven

and fear Hell. Watch the man that believes in
God, and yet while in health refuses to obey
him; watch him going through life cussing and
lieing and stealing and drinking; watch him
when he falls on a bed of sickness, and when he
thinks he is going to die listen to his mournful
cries to God for help; and after he thinks he is
going to die, if it should turn out that he was
mistaken and he gets well, watch him; in two
months afterwards he'll be nearer than ever.
The fellow that works for the devil all of his life
may think he'll get a crown and a harp for hol-
lering between the last breath and death, "Oh
God have mercy on my soul," but he'll come
nearer getting horns and a forked tail.

I once saw a man die accusing surrounding
circumstances of sending him to Hell, a scene I
shall never forget. He was brought up in a
Christian home; all of the surroundings of his
youth were calculated to make a noble man and
after he grew up his star of the future was brilliant with promise. One evening he was going
to prayer meeting and met an old acquaintance
that had just returned from the West. The acquaintance insisted on him going to a saloon and
taking a drink just for the sake of old times.
After a good deal of persuasion his resolution
gave way and he went—went through the door
of earth's hell and drank damnation at its coun-

ter just for the sake of old times, and from that moment on church and song and prayer lost their charm, surrounding circumstances were changed—changed for that man forever. The home of his childhood was no longer interesting and even the poor old gray-haired mother who had nursed him in sickness and humored him in health could no longer persuade him to spend his evenings at home with her. His old associates dropped off one by one and drunken, tough rowdies of the town took their place, and at last whisky took entire possession of his being. A robbery was committed, suspicion pointed her unfeeling finger at him, and in order to keep out of the penitentiary he had to run away from the only home in the whole wide world that would offer him a cheerful welcome. I met him the first time on the borders of the west, he was in rags and almost starving. I took pity on him and used my influence to get him a position as a cowboy on a large cattle ranch. He led a daring, reckless life, apparently neither afraid of man or devil, but at last in a drunken row he was shot just over the heart. He lingered several days. I was with him in his dying hours, and he told me of his home, his old gray-haired father and mother, of the bright prospects of his youth, of the circumstance that caused his fall. His father and mother were both dead, they died with broken hearts. In a little cabin without the slightest comfort, away out on one of the large prairies of the West that boy that was raised in luxury, who while in youth sipped every comfort from the cup of life, lay on a dirty blanket spread on a ground floor, caring nothing for his physical pain although it was great. At times he would look back into the past with tears of remorse coursing down his palid cheeks and blame surrounding circumstances for his sufferings. At last when death drew nearer this man that was considered so brave in health, became one of the greatest cowards I ever saw. It seemed that he was looking straight through the open gates of hell; he would strain and jerk and roll and scream and beg, until death came and opened up an avenue of escape for his tortured soul. As I stood with tearful eyes and bowed head over the yet warm remains of that reckless boy, I thought of all of the early opportunities of the good surroundings of this youth and how he had ignored them. I thought of the false friend, the first drink. I thought of God and the Holy Bible, but on its sacred pages I could not remember of ever seeing a single word of hope for that lost soul that had sought circumstances to hurry it on to eternal doom.

STRAY SHOTS AT THE DEVIL.

We may travel all of our life in every way possible. Over every country of this entire globe. We may sleep on the hard rock of privation in the house of bitter want and mingle with fortune's favorites in the parlors of sumptuous fashion. During all of our experience we will never be able to find in the human race anything but people. Some are bad and others are worse; some are good and others are better; but for all of that a Christian is a Christian and a sinner is a sinner—the one does not blend into the other. We cannot be both at the same time. There are many bad church members, but there are no bad Christians. There are many good sinners, but the best sinner on earth is not near so good as a genuine Christian.

I never saw a man in all of my life whom I thought was too mean to have a streak of goodness running through his character. Neither did I ever see a man whom I thought was too good to have a small spark of meanness somewhere in his composition. Although we are mostly different in many things we are generally alike. The same cold that would freeze a Gould would freeze a pauper and the same fire that would warm one would warm the other.

The aspirations of a millionaire are generally different from those of a poor man, and yet if the millionaire's stomach was empty he would have the same desire for something to eat that the poor man has.

The poor laborer works for bread, while the rich millionaire works for railroads. Make the poor man rich and he will begin to think about railroads. Make the rich man poor and he will begin to think about bread.

Extremes are dangerous, too much heat will burn and too much cold will freeze.

Extreme poverty and extreme wealth often prove a curse to mankind. Great wealth stimulates selfishness and great poverty creates bitterness. While there are exceptions I would seek pure unselfish Christianity in that home where the wolf of want and the butterfly of fashion are strangers.

Poverty is not a blessing for this earth neither is riches; the one may be a misfortune the other is positively a responsibility.

Many people admire riches, I don't. I admire character. I would just as soon shake hands with a pauper as a millionaire. I would just as soon see the poorest person in this town go to Heaven as the richest. We must remember that God is no respecter of persons.

If some great capitalist would come to this town and offer to put up a large distillery or brewery, one that would employ several hundred hands, there are some old gray haired money grabbers that belong to the church that would do all in their power to get the Hell making machine in this place. Some of them would be willing to spend a great deal of money before they would let the offer fall through. And why? I'll tell you. They think their business interests would be benefited, or that their property would increase in value.

They are enemies of the Devil until he offers them a bribe, and then they become his best friends. Some of them have children growing up. Some of them have boys, and they want lots of money to leave them when they die.

A few distilleries and breweries and saloons will do the work. Business will boom; they will get rich. But while business is booming drunkenness will boom, crime will boom, and Hell will boom. They will get rich while the distilleries and breweries are puffing and spewing alcohol of damnation for the souls of their boys and friends and neighbors. I don't weigh but one hundred and twenty pounds, but I'm not afraid to tell such church members what they are. They are traitors to God and traitors to earth. They are traitors to the early teachings of their devoted Christian mothers. They are treacherous, lieing hypocrites. The few paltry dollars they give the church they give begrudgingly, little caring or thinking that it is worth more to them and theirs than all of the whisky making and Devil-breeding machines on earth could ever be.

If I have fired shot into the camp of the Devil, I have no apology to make. When you shoot at a hog, if you don't hit him he is not likely to squeal. The caps that I throw out in this audience are only intended for those that find a fit, and whoever finds a fit is perfectly welcome to it.

All of my ammunition is for the devil and I'm determined to shoot it in that direction. I don't care what kind of clothes he wears, jeans or broadcloth, I would just as soon spoil one as the other. If I can take any of the polish off of a dude's shoes and put it on his heart I'll do it. I've got a good recipe for making a dude, I'll tell it to you: Take a worm-eaten peg and fill the worm hole with the brain of a common house fly, glue the peg to a rotten Irish potato, use four tooth picks for legs and arms, dress in the latest dude fashion with an exceedingly flashy necktie. The result will be a dude of the first family.

A dude is a tobacco consuming animal with clothes on, useless to every one but the manufacturer of cigarettes. Its life is wasted on the street corners and in front of churches as people go in and out.

The dude is indigenous to most countries and places, but flourishes better in large cities. You havn't got any dudes in this place. They are imitations and the imitation don't last long, for they soon learn that to be a dude we must be born one, and to be born a dude is a mistake of nature, as a dude's parents are frequently very respectable people.

It is not the kind of clothes you wear that makes you a dude, but the way you wear them. Wear all of the fine clothes you will, if you can afford it, but don't let your clothes come between you and God. Don't be stuck up; don't think that you are any better in your broadcloth than your neighbor is in his jeans.

Clothes may make dudes, but they don't make men, men make clothes. Whenever I think about a dude I think about the ball room, not because all people that dance are dudes, but because nearly all dudes dance.

When I think about the ball room I think about Hell.

I believe that it would be a great surprise to

many church members to know how many people have danced themselves to Hell.

If the Devil ever had a chance to wreck a woman's life and soul he has it in the ball room. Mothers and fathers if you have any regard for the purity of your daughters, trust them to a den of rattlesnakes rather than in the nicest of the unbridled passions of the Devil's whirl. Any member of the Methodist or Presbyterian church that do dance or encourages it in any way is guilty of perjury.

I would rather wear the stripes of the convict that was sent to the penitentiary for perjury than to wear the stripes that some church members will have to wear in Hell for the same crime. A man with a church membership without religion is a hypocrite that reminds me of a snake—it's hard to tell where the tail ends and the body begins.

People that smile and sing and pray in church and frown and fuss and almost fight at home, havn't got enough religion to float them a half a mile towards Heaven. They are all wind; they might do for a blacksmith's bellows, but they don't do for a Christian. If you have a home, make the best of it. A Christian's home unites Earth with Heaven and is the one sacred spot where the early teachings of the devoted mother opens the heart of infantile innocence and gives purity a resting place through the whole of life.

Early training is the most lasting—good fruit trees come from good nurseries. They require the training and the grafting, and so it is with people. Train them right in their childhood; graft the religion of Jesus Christ in their hearts as they grow—some of them may sprout hell-wards, but the sprouts are easy to trim. They are not hard to reclaim and caused to bear the most luscious fruits of Christianity. Oh! fathers and mothers if you love God and Heaven. If you would have your children with you forever, make your home what this church is, a House of God. Sing there as you do here; pray there as you do here. Be as careful about what you do and say there as you are here. Childish laughter and innocent amusement should not be disturbed by frowns and quarrels of parents. But be sure that the amusement is innocent, not only in your own home but any home that your children may desire to visit.

Guard your children from sin as you would guard them from small pox. Shield them from every temptation that your experience has taught you to be dangerous. Hundreds of boys are on the road to Hell and the carelessness of their parents is frequently the cause of it.

Hundreds of girls are leading a life of shame, because their parents gave the Devil every opportunity to ruin them.

Did I say Devil? Yes, and I repeat it. Devil. Hellish Devil would sound better, for that man that would wreck the life and soul of innocent, confiding womanhood, is a traitor to his race, reeking with the vermin of Hell, more to be feared than the rattlesnake, and deserves to be shot down like a mad dog in the streets. The murderer pays the penalty of his crime on the gallows, while his victim sleeps peacefully in the grave. But the murderer of a woman's purity is often petted by society, while his victim suffers and festers in the filth of prostitution. Next to God, I love my wife and children. I have a little girl hardly three years old. Oh! what a treasure is my little sweetheart baby girl; I often get a glimpse of Heaven in her dancing eyes. Her childish laughter sounds to me like the music of angels. I look on her as a gift from Heaven. I feel that I love her as much as God ever permits a man to love his child. Were it not for my love of Christ and faith in God, her death would be to me a heart-twisting sorrow beyond my endurance, and yet I would see her dead and buried ten thousands of times before I would have her grow up and fall in the lustful arms of prostitution, and I believe every father and mother in this house will endorse my sentiments.

Mothers, how many sleepless nights have you

spent over the sick cradle of your children?
How many silent tears have you shed over their
sorrows? How much have you worked and
suffered and sacrificed for their sake? How
great is your ambition for their happiness? Do
you wish to see them disgraced for earth and
ruined for Hell? No, no, no! In tones of thun-
der, no! Every pulsation of your heart throws
your real life's blood against the phonograph of
your mind and thrills your entire being with the
one word, no! To see the darlings of your heart
in the fermenting vat of iniquity would cause
you to shed bloody tears of almost unconsolable
sorrow, and yet some of you have children that
are standing on the very brink of destruction,
and you sit with folded arms and sleeping energy, while your child prepares for the fatal
leap. There is a mighty wreck close at hand;
the safe bridge of Christianity is torn away; the
train of life is hurrying on faster and faster,
nearer and nearer. Wake up, you sleepy parents; hurry with the danger signal; wave your
flag high in the air if you would save your children from a wild and reckless plunge into the
muddy river of sin and Hell.

Make your homes as pure and pleasing as
possible, turn every quarrel into a prayer. Pray
for your children—with your children. Try to
keep them out of bad company. Remember

birds of a feather flock together. Keep your children away from the buzzards of crime, if you don't want them to eat of the rotten carcass of sin.

Stand bravely under the cross of Christ, if you would have pure homes and good children. Never let an opportunity to do good slip into the past unnoticed. The bullets that you shoot the Devil with must be made out of the religion of Jesus Christ, they are the only kind that will kill sin. Keep your gun loaded and whenever and wherever the Devil shows himself shoot. Keep him out of your home even if he wears broadcloth or satin.

If you teach your children right ninety-nine times out of a hundred they will teach their children right. Oh, that every father and every mother would plant the flowers of Christianity in their home and cultivate them through the whole of life. How sweet would be the perfumes of consolation, and how joyous would be the meeting in the end of time on the golden streets of musical Heaven. Father and mother, daughter and son, grandchildren and great grandchildren, all with God and together forever and forever, beyond the trials and cares and sorrows of earth, in the home sweet home of Heaven, built on the rock of eternal ages. There every heart will throb with pleasure, every smile will grow into happy laughter, which will go flashing on against the chords of eternity and cause them to vibrate into divine symphonies that will thrill the heart of every angel with perpetual joy.

A TEMPERANCE TALK.

The most profitable business of the Devil is the saloon. Alcohol is God's worst enemy and the Devil's best friend. The most of the crimes of civilization are turned through the faucets of the whisky barrel. The saloons are seeds of sin from which grow saplings and trees of crime, that are eventually washed into the furnaces of Hell by the briney tears of poverty, oppressed widows and orphans. Through the microscope of truth we can see in every glass of strong drink the heart of the Devil that ofttimes gives strength to the arm of the midnight murderer to plunge a blade of steel into the heart of his sleeping victim. More tears of sorrow have been shed over the drunken carcass of alcohol than the world could count in an entire lifetime.

Behind the screen of every saloon there is a den of hissing, writhing snakes that are continually striking their sharp fangs in the flesh of innocence and poisoning it with vice.

As we float down the river of life we see on the right hand churches and godliness, cleanliness and prosperity, and we see on the left saloons and drunkenness and filth and misery and poverty.

He that buys whisky buys his own misery and the misery of those that love him, and he that sells it snatches bread and meat from the mouths of defenseless women and helpless children. Better far sell rough on rats and arsenic for they only poison the body and do the work quick, while whisky gives a lingering life of misery and poisons the soul for the eternal torments of Hell.

He that casts his vote in favor of whisky is a traitor to his friends and an enemy to his own children. It is the duty of every Christian father and mother and son and daughter to deal with whisky as they would with a poisonous snake. Crush it wherever you see it, it is always coiled and ready to strike.

If a mad dog was running through this town, men would run for their guns. If ten thousand mad dogs were running and biting as they went, they could not do as much harm as one saloon.

One soul in Hell will suffer more in a year than this whole place could suffer from bites from all of the mad dogs that ever lived. If the church members of this town would put their hearts and heads together and fight whisky with the same force that they would mad dogs they would soon blot every saloon from the map of this place.

Oh, says old bald-headed hypocrite, I would vote against whisky, but then you see, my friend runs a saloon and, besides, I am in the mercantile business, and if the sale of liquor was prohibited here it would hurt my business. People would go to some other town to trade. You are but another Judas selling Jesus Christ for a few pieces of silver. While you are thinking of your friend that deals in liquor you are forgetting your children and your other friends and their children. You are not with our Savior, who said: "He that is not with me is against me." You are one of the Devil's agents pushing your own children down the road to destruction.

Says Mr. Dram Drinker, I can't see any harm in an occasional drink, just so a man don't make a hog of himself. Therefore, although I am a church member, I vote for it. Yes, you are a church member, and that is all—you are certainly not a Christian. You know that there are hundreds of people that do make hogs of themselves, and that every town in every state where liquor is sold look on drunkenness as a nuisance. Although the town will issue license for the whisky seller it will also issue warrants for the whisky drinker.

The Indians of this country are treated as wards of the government and the traffic of intoxicating liquors is positively prohibited among the nations of the Indian Territory; and yet this self same government sells its permission for liquor to be sold in the states. If it is a crime to murder in California it is a crime to murder in Kentucky. If it is a crime to sell whisky in the Indian Territory it is a crime to sell it in the States, and should be punished in all places alike. It is not only the drunkards that suffer, but thousands of wives and children are compelled to receive curses and bruises from husband and father instead of bread and meat, and it is not only the saloon keeper that is responsible for this state of affairs, every man that casts his vote in favor of whisky or fails to cast his vote and influence against it, is on the side of whisky and is helping the Devil to starve women and children. Those that are with whisky are heaping stones of sorrow on the back of poverty and crowding the poor house and prisons of the country with victims of vice that grew from seeds of purity.

This country is full of rags and dirt and misery in the very midst of plenty, and absolute prohibition is the only thing that will dry up the tears of poverty and wash and clothe its dirt-polluted body.

If you desire to do a deed of charity work with all of your might and main against the vile fiends of Hell, and every mother and wife and child that are the innocent victims of drunken-ness will wipe the tears of sorrow from the eyes of love and thank you a thousand times from the very depths of their overjoyed hearts. Work and pray to God to crown your work with suc-cess, and you will see good clothes take the place of rags; you will see the waters of prohibition wash the dirt from the tear-stained face of pov-erty; you will hear songs of praise to God in that house where you now hear oaths and screams of anguish. Although I hate alcohol and its evils, I do not hate the saloon keeper and his patrons. I pity the barkeeper and the drunkard from the very bottom of my heart. I love all men; they are my brothers, and if they fall in the slimy pool of iniquity I am ever ready with all of my strength to help them up. Oh! how my heart aches to see my brothers in life sell their souls for gold or sell their mother's comfort and wives and children's happiness and their own souls for strong drink.

Mothers and wives and sisters and sweethearts, for God's sake and your sake, I plead with you with tears of emotion flowing from a pain swelling heart. Pray and work as you never prayed and worked before. Yes, pray and work and persuade in church and on the streets and in your homes, for Christ's sake and your father's sake and your brother and husband and sweetheart's sake and your own sake. Pray and work and cry and plead for the death of the burning curse of mankind. Your happiness is at stake, the happiness of those you love is in danger. Pure, noble women, you are the angels of earth. Your influence is great; your sweet Christian care and your gentle loving words begin with us at the cradle—let them last to the grave. Good Christians are often made at home by the early teachings of the loving mother, the noble attributes of man were cultivated by the lips of the mother while he laid in her lap smiling and cooing in infantile innocence. Woman, man is indebted to you for his early training, and unless whisky has completely drowned his self-respect and turned him into a brute, he will listen to your tearful entreaties and determine to become a respectable human. Without your aid the ship of Prohibition is lost. You by nature know the way to man's heart; reach it, and God will reform your drunken father, husband, son or sweetheart. Work, work, work! so that the pest will become a hideous nightmare on the tablets of memory, so that in the near future there may be a glorious rally over the festering carcass of dead alcohol. Let your prayers to God be long and strong and full of tears, so that in the future they may be full of the smiles of thanksgiving. You can't vote, but in the end one prayer is worth more than a hundred votes. Not since the morning stars first sang together and the sons of God laughed for joy has noble woman had more influence than now. And if you will only use it with the force of undying determination, all that sell and drink will fall at the feet of Christ and beg God for forgiveness. If we could only wean the drunken calves that suck their crimes from the breasts of alcohol, there would be a smile for every tear, a joy for every sorrow, a prayer for every oath and a song to God for every bruise. The Devil would cover his face with shame and slink back into the darkest corners of Hell. Earth would be an Eden before the fall of Adam and the reign of Christ would be absolute. Oh! friends, for the sake of your dear old sacrificing, gray-haired mothers, for the sake of your loving wives and sisters and daughters, turn your hearts to Christ and here and now renounce intoxicating drinks in all of its Devil-tempting forms. When you look at it you look at ruin; cold, desolate ruin.

What man in this house is so weak as to be unable to leave the side of ruin? Who will prove his determination and set an example for Christ's sake? Who will here in public show his desire to fight the liquor traffic by standing up?

HYPOCRISY.,

The lights of Christianity are burning and blazing and growing all over this entire globe. The world is becoming greater and grander and better; every sermon in every Christian pulpit, and every prayer in every home is driving lawlessness and crime back farther and farther. Atheist and Infidel, Agnostic and Heathen are joining the Holy Pilgrimage for good and forever. The Gods of Idolatry are decaying and crumbling under the pressure of Christianity; churches are being built where saloons and gambling houses and dens of prostitution once stood, but in the midst of growing good and dying evil we occasionally see the poisonous fangs of hypocrisy reeking with the blood of many victims. We see this deceitful creature in the home spun rags of poverty and the finest silken fabrics of wealth, with the face of an angel and a tongue of the Devil. It flaunts itself into our presence while on the streets or in our homes. It even dares to take the Holy Sacrament in the House of God. Woe unto he or she that wears the mask of religion for the sake of earthly prosperity. Woe unto that man who will give fifty dollars in public to convert heathens in Asia, and will refuse to give five cents in private to feed starving widows and orphans in America. Woe unto that woman that would make the House of God a social institution, who in the silks and satins of riches will snub her nose at the rags of poverty; and on bended knees, while her lips are ostensibly moving in prayer, will envy her neighbor the bonnet she wears, and say to herself I'll have one that will beat that next Sunday.

Many heathens wear the cloak of religion. In Asia they worship the golden calf. In America they worship the golden dollar. Many pray to God in public and worship mammon in private; and of all the heathens they are the worst. If I had words in my vocabulary that would sound like the hiss of a snake or the snarl of the hyena or the grinding of the jaws of the crocodile, I could better express the contempt I have for hypocrisy. As I loathe hypocrisy I pity the hypocrite. Had I words of sorrow that would sound like the dull thud of clods falling on the coffin lid of death I would be more able to express my feelings for those that feed on the bitter plains of deceit. The rattlesnake will shake his rattlers and give you warning of your danger, but the hypocrite will take you on surprise.

In the rosiest peach we ofttimes find a worm. I once heard of an old negro that went out in the woods to get a piece of timber out of which he intended to make his wife a bread tray. He selected the straightest and apparently best tree in the forest, but while cutting it down he discovered it to be hollow. That is what is the matter with some of you church members, you are all right on the outside, but your hearts are hollow, the disease of deceit has rotted out the core. Deceitful Judas betrayed Christ with a kiss—the most deadly poison is frequently as sweet as honey. Is the poisonous honey of Christ's betrayer on your lips? Do you carry the hypocrisy-permeated heart of Judas in your breast? Are you a wolf in sheep's clothing, seeking the flesh and blood of mutilated innocence? A traitor to God, a traitor to earth, a traitor to yourself. Hypocrisy is born of the womb of envy and selfishness, and is a bridle in the hands of the Devil, that drives thousands of souls to Hell. The curse of God made the snake the common enemy of mankind from the very beginning of creation, and yet should I meet one in the road by the side of foul-mouthed hypocrisy I would place more confidence in the snake than I would the hypocrite.

How often do we see the trap of hypocrisy baited with the tempting bread of deceit, luring game of innocence into hell dens of vice. How often have I heard this man or that woman say, I would try to become a Christian, but what is the use, I'd just as soon be a professed sinner as to be like old Mr. Skin Flint; he'll go to church and pray all day Sunday and then go home and study the whole of next week every way and every means by which he may swindle poor widows and orphans out of their inheritance. How often have I heard it said that fashionable Mrs. Society belongs to the church, and will throw up her hands with holy horror at the mere thought of going to a circus or theatre, and will blush with indignation at the bare mention of tights, but still this fashionable Mrs. Society will go to the seashore and put on tights and swim around for fun. I tell you I've got more respect for the woman that wears tights under a canvas on a trapeze bar for a living than I have for the church member that wears them on the seashore for fun.

Some preacher goes wrong and the Devil claps his hands with hellish glee, and every sinner begins to cast slurs at the church, as though the church was responsible for the sins of man. I will admit that a mean preacher is the meanest thing on earth. However, if every preacher and every member of every church was swimming in the filthy blood of crime that would be no proof against the doctrines of Christianity—the holy word of God. Every house stands on its own foundation. Every man is responsible to God for his own acts. Let the teachings of Christ be your guide and not the frailties of mankind. Do not laugh and gloat over the sins of others, for by so doing you are kindling the fires of hell for yourself; rather let tears of sorrow flow from a heart of pity. Fall on your knees and beg God to pour the Divine oil of His mercy into their sin-rushing hearts and cause them to beat and throb with penitence. We should strive to make the holy word of God our guide through the whole of life. Our conscience is ofttimes very treacherous. Conscience is in fact a creation of education and will not do to trust. I remember when I was a small boy I had a grand and noble Christian mother. The little infantile prayer she taught me, "Now lay me down to sleep, I pray Thee, oh Lord, my soul to keep," will not be erased from the tablets of my memory as long as I breathe the air of life. The first oath that I ever swore caused my conscience to ache and

bleed with pain, the second did not hurt quite
so bad and the third was still less troublesome.
Finally I could swear all day long without being
troubled at all.   Crime will soon harden and
callous the most tender conscience. The first sin
creates a blister, the second lets the water out,
the third hardens it and so on until a hardened
corn of sin protrudes from the once tender foot
of innocent conscience. And I tell you such
corns are like any other corns, extremely hard
to cure, but there is a remedy that is certain to
give relief and will sooner or later give a permanent cure to the most obstinate case.   It was
patented in Heaven and its trade mark is prayer.
Use it freely and the skin of your conscience will
become as soft as down and as tender as the rosy
cheeks of healthy infancy. The hardest nut I
ever cracked contained a small, but extremely
sweet kernel.   If the meanest old reprobate in
this house would take the hammer of prayer
and crack open that old hardened hickory nut
that beats in his breast which he calls heart he
would find a sweet kernel of goodness that would
grow and permeate his whole being with the religion of Jesus Christ. Small seed grow into
little saplings and little saplings grow into large
trees. Short prayers grow into longer ones and
long prayers grow into good Christian men and
women. My sinning friend I am not preaching

to wound your feelings—far from that. I do
not hate the man that has the consumption, I
hate the consumption; I do not hate the sinner,
I hate his sins. I love you, I pity you. I care
not who you are nor where you are from, this
world is my country and every human being in
every land is my kindred, We all have the
blood of old Grandfather Adam flowing in our
veins. Nothing causes my heart to swell with
greater sorrow than the death of a lost sinner.
Nothing permeates my entire being with greater
joy than the conversion of a sinner into a lamb
of God. I am standing on the seashore of safety
and I see a huge ship loaded with human freight
in the midst of the winds and storms of sin. All
of the passengers of that ship are my brothers
and sisters. Oh, God! how my mind is racked
and tortured. I see the huge rocks of death
protruding through the storm-lashed waves of
life. Not a man aboard of that ship seems to
know how to steer into the bay of safety. I
know the right course. No wonder I preach and
cry and beg and pray; my sinning brothers and
sisters are aboard of that ship. Oh! I can see it
now as it strikes the dark rocks of death. See
it bend, hear it crack. Brother, sister, jump in
the lifeboat of Christ's love, or all is lost. Struggling and dying and sinking into the fathomless
depths of Hell will be the history of all that re-

main. Oh, my sinner friends steer your ship into the bay of Christ and all will be saved. Saved from Hell; saved for God and Heaven and eternity.

A TALK.

Ofttimes man is educated to believe that which is untrue. Generally his religious belief is engrafted into his mind when a mere child, and even if wrong if he proves his faith in his religion by his works, God will give him his reward.

I would rather be a heathen on my knees grovel.ng in the mud and mire in the hot, sultry climate of India, worshiping a dried snake and proving my belief in that snake by my works, than to be a member of the best church of Christendom trying to roll into glory on the car of faith without the engine of good works to push me. Because you are a member of a certain church and go to that church every Sunday, is no proof that you are a Christian. To act a Christian while in church and then go home and fuss about this thing, or that thing, or speak disrespectfully of the dress that Mrs. So and So wore, may fool some people, but in the great

day of judgment you will find that God was not
so easy fooled. Some people have got more religion in their clothes than they have in their
hearts. When they put on their Sunday-go-to-
meeting clothes, they put on a long, pious look
with them and become apparent Christians for
one day, but as soon as they take off their
clothes and hang them up on a nail, they hang
all of the religion they ever had up with them.

I don't care how much faith you have in Jesus
Christ, if you don't prove your faith by obeying
his commandments you are a lost sinner, and to
obey the commandments of our Lord should not
be a task but a pleasure. To carry the cross of
Christ is the best job you ever had, and in the
final day of judgment you will receive your
wages in the legal tender of God's mercy, which
will be worth more than all of the wealth of the
Vanderbilts and the Goulds and the Astors
and the entire Globe.

I've heard some church members say it is
mighty hard to be a Christian with all of the
trials and cares they had. Poor, deluded, miserable sinners complaining of the cross of Christ,
and claiming to be one of God's chosen, in their
efforts to deceive God, they deceive themselves.
They mistake ceremony for Christianity.

Show me a genuine Christian (none of your
long, owl-faced hypocrites) and I will show you

a truly happy man or woman. Sinners never know what genuine happiness is; when they are too good to commit great crimes, little ones hurt their conscience; and when they are hardened criminals fear of the law, penitentiary and gallows keep them miserable.

Extract all of the vanity and prejudice and party spirit from the religion of some church members, and they would not have enough Christianity left to fill the skull of a mosquito.

The cross that Christ carried is not the cross that you will have to carry. Christ clothed in the flesh of man, feeling, hearing, smelling, tasting and seeing as man suffered more for us than our mind is capable of understanding. Christ struggling and fainting under the weight of a wooden cross, bleeding and dying for the salvation of mankind, is a picture that we have all been accustomed to look at with reverence from the cradle up.

The nails driven in the feet and hands, the sword thrust in the side, were but one drop of sorrow in the bucket of Christ's life. It was his mind that was tore and hacked and cut. It was not the red life's blood flowing from his physical wounds that gave him so much anguish. It was the blood of compassion flowing from the wounds of His Godly mind, produced by the nails and swords of sin.

The Jews crucified Christ and every sinner of every land have been carrying on the bloody butchery through many ages of the past until the present. Every sin we commit we drive a nail in the cross of Christ, and sinners if you don't watch out it will be so full of nails from your driving that you will not have time to pull them out before the cold, clammy hand of death wi.l close your eyelids in perpetual earthly sleep, and your soul is hurled into the bottomless pits of eternal sorrow. God does not only require that we should be good, but that we should do good. Do good wherever and whenever an opportunity presents itself, and if opportunities don't come to you, go to them. Make all of the prayers you can in public, and make ten in private for every one you make in public, but never ask God to do something for you that you are able, but unwilling, to do for yourself.

Some people are too lazy to work; and they are always begging God for something to eat. You see such people in every church. They appear solemn, and are always talking about what good Christians they are. They are lazy and hungry and do more harm in the church than they would out of it. If they would go to work and fill their stomach and smile and laugh a little they would perhaps become happy Christians.

Don't let any unchristian act be your guide; don't say Mr. or Mrs. So and So belong to the church and do certain little things that are wrong, and I guess I will do them too. If you want to be a good Christian do what you think a good Christian ought to do. Don't think that because others sin it gives you a license to sin— every tub stands on its own bottom—if it has got any. Every man is responsible for his own sins, if he has got any mind, and if he hasn't he is all right, for he will get an idiot's passport to Heaven. Heaven, Heaven! What a sweet word, sweeter than all of the words framed with the letters of all of the alphabets of all of the languages of this entire globe, and oh, so full of joyful meaning. Home, sweet home, a home of rest; a home of comfort; a home of joy; a home with God; a home where we will meet our father and our sweet, dear old mother. There her sweet face will not be tear-stained and pale and wrinkled, but will be blooming with the red roses of eternal health and happiness. The waters of the divine love of Jesus Christ will wash out all remembrance of sorrow. And oh, what a grand jubilee we will have when we meet our loved ones on the Golden Streets of God's home and your home and my home. We will not have a jubilee of one day, but forever and forever. Old gray-haired mothers and old bald-headed fathers, don't think so much about your children's future on earth; think more of their future in eternity. You have toiled and suffered and economized all through your married life; and for what? For money—money to leave your children when you die—and it is likely to do them more harm than good. Children raised on a golden spoon, often die with a brass one in their mouth. Raise your children well and then let them make their own spoons, and ninety-nine times out of a hundred they will be better than any that you can give. Feed them on the milk of Christianity and they will grow up to noble manhood and womanhood. A Christian's deed to a home in Heaven is worth more to you and your children than all you will ever be able to make or see on earth.

Mothers, do you remember when your little dancing-eyed, sunny-haired child was sick—almost dying? Oh! how you watched and nursed and prayed, and when the doctor said there was no hope, your heart throbbed and pained so that even the tears of sorrow could not flow, and when all earthly hope was gone God answered your prayers and performed a miracle even as Christ performed while in the flesh. The hot and parching fever vanished and your little darling grew back into health. That child is perhaps grown now: grown and on the road to ruin and you seem contented. Your child was saved for this world. Well in the body, but sick and dying in the mind, the spirit, the soul. Now is the time to sorrow and pray. Oh, God! I beg of Thee as I never begged before. Give, oh give me thoughts and words that will flash like powder when touched by fire. Yes, flash and burn into the hearts and souls of every Christian father and every Christian mother in this house. Flash and burn into energy and zeal and cause them to go to work in dead earnest, work and struggle and pray for their children and friends and neighbors, for many of them are sick and dying.

Yes, my friends, many of you are sick and dying; and your burning, torturing, agonizing disease is sin, cold, heartless, contagious sin, worse than small pox and cholera and yellow fever, for they only open the avenues of the soul and allow it to pass into the eternal future.

Sin is a slimy, crawling, treacherous snake that works and hisses in us and out of us and around us, until we are contorted and twisted and poisoned in both mind and body and turned into fuel for Hell.

The wages of sin are so great that it is astonishing to me that every sinner in every land do not fall on their knees and beg God for mercy and forgiveness.

Oh, my sinning friend! lost, lost, lost! is written with big, bloody letters of sin across your name, but the letters are not indelible. You, by the help of Christ, can erase them. Christ lived to save you, Christ died to save you, Christ is, and has, and will, ever be ready to extend you a helping hand. For Christ's sake, for your good, old mother's sake, for your father's sake -- for the sake of all that you love, throw yourself at the feet of Christ, repent of your sins and beg God for mercy. God is merciful. Heaven is full of mercy. Open your heart to God and Christ will fill it with the wine of love from the fountain of mercy.

Oh! that the heart-wringing word of lost would be blotted here and now, so that saved might be written in its place.

Saved for father, saved for mother, saved for earth, saved for Heaven, saved for eternity, saved for God.

THE HOLY BIBLE.

This is the Holy Bible, the book of books from
God through man to man, a history of the beginning, a prophesy of the end—a record of war
and famine and pestilence and flood.   A champion of truth and love and justice and mercy, a
fulfillment of prophecy, printed in every language. taught in every country.   Go where you
will over North and South America, Europe,
Asia, Africa and Australia, and almost every in-
habited island of every ocean and sea and lake
and river.   You will find this most precious of
all books unchangeable and indesructibly printed
with the indelible ink of God's mercy—bathed
in the blood of Jesus Christ, made holy by all
of the pains and aches and sorrows of martyrdom.   When a storm-tossed, wave-washed ship
bends, breaks and sinks under the mighty fury
of the elements, the sailor boy that in the midst
of cries and curses and prayers holds close to his
heart the Bible his dying mother gave him long
ago, may go down to the bottom of the mighty
deep with the rest, but his mother, an angel in
Heaven, will look on—not with sorrow—but
with joy, for her darling boy will be saved—not

for earth, but for God and her and Heaven.

When the misfortunes of earth come to us furious, thick and fast, if we open this sacred book and read we will be comforted. It is permeated with hope and peace and promise. If our mind is weak we will find simplicity on every page; if our mind is strong we will find depth in every chapter. This is a book of law from the very fountain of law. Read, believe and obey if you would be happy on earth and in eternity. There are perhaps in this book many things that we do not understand, and yet those things that are essential to our salvation are very plain. Voltair's have ridiculed, Tom Paine's have reasoned and Ingersoll's have lectured. The atheist, infidel and deist have laughed at the miracles herein recorded. Poor finite minds laughing at the mysteries of God, incapable of understanding the great mystery of life and death, unable to understand the miracles that occur every day. Such as the growth of a small seed into a large tree; unable to understand the law of like producing like; unable to explain the control of mind over matter; trying to steal from the human race all hope and all consolation and all harm, and giving nothing in return but cold, silent, perpetual death. Give the reins of your belief into the hands of the atheist and he will drive you to death, de-

struction and Hell.   Make the Holy Bible your
guide, and it will lead you to the green pastures
and floral gardens of endless joy.   Destroy this
book and you will destroy every Christian
church in every land, and erase from the mind
of every devoted child the early teachings of the
loving mother.   Civilization would fall back
into heathenism and barbarity.   Morality and
justice would bleed and die in the clutches of
vice.   Hell for earth, Hell forever.   The purity
of the marriage tie, home comfort and fireside
are built on the sacred truths of this Holy book.
Take it away and you tear the foundation from
the house of all that is good and it will crumble,
totter and fall into the slimy quagmires of sin.

Shakspeare is a great book, and yet if another
were born to the world every year for ten thous-
and of years, and the next would always be better than the last; the whole would not be
worth as much to the world as one line of this
Holy word of God.   Every promise in this book
is from the creator of all things and every promise will be fulfilled.   Without the Bible every
pleasure has its sorrow; within the Bible every
sorrow has its pleasure.   Judge the tree by its
fruit—the seed of the thorns brings forth thorns.
Viciousness sprouts from the roots of vice.   It
is in the saloons and gambling dens and filthy
places of prostituted iniquity where the seeds of

crime are first planted. With this book in this church or any other church, in the home of every Christian father and every Christian mother, the seeds of ‚truth and love and virtue are sown and cultivated, and they grow in the sunshine of God's mercy and bring forth God-loving, Devil-hating, noble men and women.

Your homes and your property, your mother and your sister and your wife are protected by the law, and law does not come from the lawless, it comes from the good and just. All goodness and all justice are taught by the sacred chapters of this Holy book. Civilization was built up by its teachings, and would fade, famish and die without it. Show me a home with the Bible where Christian father and mother and sister and brother read and pray together, and I'll show you a home of love and sympathy and forbearance beautified with the sunshine of happiness and Godliness. A home without the Bible may cost ever so much furnished in the most elaborate style, and yet in that home you will find the hydra-headed monster of deceit and selfishness. In sickness and death you will see the cross-bones and eyeless skull of buried hope. For that home there is no happiness beyond death. There you will find butterflies of vanity drinking poisons of Hell from the golden cup of arrogant wealth. The time is sure to come when

beauty will fade and misery will wear the crown
—wealth will vanish and the pauper despair
will carry the scepter. For you that believe
and obey, the time is sure to come when every
sorrow will be wrung from your Christ-loving,
God-worshiping souls, and they will go on ab-
sorbing the endless pleasures of Heaven through
all eternity. For you that disbelieve or disobey
there are no words in the English language with
sufficient horror to describe the aches and pains
of your tortured souls in the fathomless ocean of
dark, burning, blistering, shrieking Hell.

Hell is not made of real fire and brimstone, it
is worse. Heaven is not made of real gold and
diamonds, it is better. There are many roads
leading to Hell. They go from every saloon
and gambling house and dance hall and race
track. They all start from the birthplace of sin.
Many start in the costly carriage of riches, but
end as paupers, begging whisky on the way.
The earthly beginning of most roads to Hell are
clear and bright. Tempting flowers of deceit
bud and blossom on either side. The further
you go the darker things grow. Your associates
become more open and bold in crime; every
flower of happiness soon fades away and your
body aches and bleeds from the thorns of dissi-
pation and vice.

A sinner and a pauper's grave is oh! so often

of giving away to the first temptation. The
earthly road to Heaven ends as it starts full of
promise, bright and clear. On either side are
the sweet roses of charity laden with the perfumes of brotherly love. No thorns of despair
but full of the heliotropes of devotion and hope,
budding and blooming into more beauty every
mile you travel. A Christian's death is the end
of sorrow; a sinner's death is the end of happiness. Oh, my sinning friends, read, believe
and obey this most Holy Book. If you would
eat of the bread of eternal life (your sins are gar-
ments of filth, breeding vermin for Hell) throw
yourself at the feet of Christ and beg God for the
divine ointment of forgiveness—wash your sinful hearts in the waters of penitence. Christ is
ready, Christ is willing, Christ is here. Come,
every Christian in this house will help you pray.
Every angel in Heaven will rejoice at your coming. Moses and Abraham and Isaac and Jacob
will sing praises to God. Come, all that is good
on Heaven and earth will laugh for joy at your
coming. The demons of sin may hiss and snarl
in the darkest corners of Hell. but come. The
Devil wants you for flame and fire and smoke;
Christ wants you for music and joy and Heaven.

CHRISTIANITY.

Christianity is all music and love and laughter and joy, permeated with everything that is good and grand and noble. In sickness and sorrow and death it gives comfort and hope. It is the salt of life, the water of civilization. It builds churches and reforms drunkards and gamblers and thieves and murderers. It drowns vice and makes the men good and the good better. It is the rudder that guides us from earth to Heaven, and without it we are ships of discontent, floating on the bitter waters of sin, without sail, without stream, without rudder, without Christ. Blown on and on by the winds and storms of bad to worse, and at last wrecked against the dark rocks of death, and left to struggle in the fiery ocean of Hell.

Brothers and sisters do not mistake a long face and hard, cold expression for religion, Christianity does not dry up the fountains of happiness, it is heartless, reckless sin that will do that. Cold, haughty, owl-faced church members have not got religion, they have dyspepsia or a liver trouble. If you want to cry, cry, don't belie your nature, don't play the hypo-

crite. God gave you eyes to see and ears to hear
and muscles to draw your lips back into laughter. Use them in a pure way wherever and
whenever you please. When you are looking at
me preach, if you see anything that makes you
feel like laughing, laugh. If you want to sleep,
sleep, but please don't snore, the person next to
you might want to sleep too. You see I want
every one to be comfortable. If what I say don't
interest you and you want to get out, get up and
go out, don't sit squirming in your seat. If
people would be just as careful about what they
do and say on the streets and at home and every
where else as they are while at church, there
would be but a little room for the Devil to work
in. "Let your light so shine before men that
they may see your good works and glorify your
Father which is in Heaven." Let your spirit
shine in church and out of church; here, there
and everywhere. Pin your faith on Jesus Christ
and do his commandments, not only on Sunday,
but every day in the week and every week in
the month and every month in the year and
every year in a lifetime. Have but one face and
let it be a Christian's face. Have but one side
to your character and let that side be good. If
you are called on to make what you deem a sacrifice for God, make it. You will find it to be
the best investment you ever made. God will

pay you with the gold of Heaven, dollar for dollar, with the biggest interest you ever heard of, and compound interest at that. The national bank of Heaven is the bank to do business with, God is its president, Christ is its cashier, and every angel in Heaven are its directors. It is loaded with the golden coin of God's mercy and Christ is ever ready to cash the checks of all. One square inch of Heaven is worth a million times more than every square mile of earth.

Men may live and men may die; nations may rise, totter and fall; war and famine and pestilence may sweep over the face of this earth, with the force of an endless tornado, yet the Bank of Heaven will stand—stand through all the years and centuries and eternity. No absconding cashier; no depreciation in stock. It is full of gold—it is made of gold. Every street leading to its doors are paved with gold. Not the gold of California and Australia, but the gold of Christ's undying love—the gold of eternal salvation.

You that love riches, throw yourself on the bosom of Christ. Pray to God for the riches of Heaven and he will make you richer than all of the emperors and kings and millionaires of earth.

The richest man in this world out of Christ is poorer than the poorest in Christ. What you have in your possession on this earth, you have borrowed, and when you die, you will have to pay it back.

If you have much, much is expected of you. The widow's mite is as great in the sight of God as the rich man's thousands. Never fear to invest your money, time or sympathy for Christ. Every investment you make for God is recorded in your favor.

When a snake raises its head to bite you will be sure to try to get out of the way, but when the Devil comes with his lying, tempting, forked tongue, many of you will allow him to insert his poisonous fangs into your very soul. More care for the body than the soul; more care for this world than the next. I tell you one minute in Heaven is worth more than a whole year on earth. One second in Hell is worse than all of the pains and sorrows of an entire lifetime. The road to Hell is a road of sin, and every mile is worse and worse and worse. The farther you travel the more weak and miserable you become. Death and fire and Hell is at the last station and you may not be ten minutes from that station. This may be your last and only chance to get on the palace car of Glory and ride on the safe road to Heaven. On this road every car is built of the timbers of promise; every rail and every tie, every screw and every nail are fastened in per-

fect place by the love of Christ. Every station
is lit up with the brilliant lights of hope. The
end is Heaven, and Heaven is eternal.

Which will you have, God and Heaven, or
the Devil and Hell? Make your choice. Eternal happiness or everlasting misery; which will
you have? Christ is the conductor for the good,
the Devil is the conductor for the bad. Both
trains are here—one goes up and the other goes
down. Everything that is great and grand and
good points to the train of Christ. Everything
that is mean and low and vicious points to the
train of the Devil. Sinners regain your self respect, wipe the tears from the wrinkled face of
your dear old mother; restore happiness to the
sorrowing heart of your sacrificing father. Make
your friends and neighbors think more of you.
Let the Devil go to Hell without you. Take the
train of Christ. It is here, ready and waiting.
Christ with outstretched hands and voice full of
compassion, preaching to a sinful world, was
working for the salvation of every living sinner.
Christ suffered on the cross of Calvary so that
you might be saved. Christ was there; the
spirit of Christ is here. It is in the heart of
every Christian in this house. It is knocking
at the door of every sinful heart in this church.

Oh, my sinning friends, open the door of
your sinful. hearts and let the Devil out and

Christ in. Throw away the bitter and rotton fruits of sin, and take from the overloaded basket of Christ's love the sweet, rich, luscious fruits of Christianity. What if your every earthly ambition was gratified, riches and health and earthly pleasures must have an end. Cold and silent death will come sooner or later. Life is but a moment hanging in all eternity. The Devil will weight your soul down to burning, shrieking Hell. Christ will raise it up to everlasting, glorious Heaven. Little Christians and big Christians; little sinners and big sinners; saloon keepers and gamblers and murderers and thieves. Christ wants all. The Devil wants all. Christ came to redeem and save the lost. I don't care how big a sinner you are, nor how big a sinner you feel yourself to be. I don't care how poor you are, nor how bad your clothes are, Christ is not afraid of poverty, he is not looking for good clothes; it is your heart; your soul that he is after. High and low, rich and poor, one soul is worth as much as another in the scales of God.

Death levels our body to an equal on earth, Christianity levels our souls to an equal in Heaven, and sin levels them to an equal in Hell. Every Christian father and every Christian mother, every Christian sister and every Christian brother, every Christian friend and every

Christian neighbor, has a heart-burning, soul-longing wish for the salvation of all of you sorrowing sinners. Because your pursuit is sin and sin means Hell, we do not dislike you; because you are a saloon keeper or gambler we do not hate you. We hate your sins and pity you. You have our sympathy. In the very midst of your sins you often do many things that are grand and noble. Your hearts would be good if you would only let them. How often have I seen a poor, starving beggar go with empty hands from the palatial home of some aristocratic church member to the hell house of a saloon keeper and extend his hand for aid. How often have I seen that saloon keeper, actuated by sympathy, reach down in his pocket and give to suffering poverty. Deeds of charity are not from the Devil. Many of you are too good to be what you are. You have been stung by the bee of sin. Eat the honey of Christian consolation and you will become brilliant lights of the church and society. Let me paint you a picture. Several years ago a large tenement house in the city of New York was burning down. The burning building was seven stories high. Away up in the attic were two little children looking out of the window crying for some one to save them. Thousands of people were congregated in front of the burning building. The firemen

had placed a huge extension ladder up against
the house. The flames were bulging out of the
windows; the walls were almost caving in. Not
a man in that whole, vast concourse of people
dared ascend the rungs of that ladder. The
mother of those poor children was coming home
from her hard days work, and as she got on the
outskirts of the crowd almost breathlessly she
looked up and saw the danger of the blue-eyed
darlings of her heart. She tried to force herself
through the almost solid mass of pitying human
beings. She tore her hair in frantic agony and
cried and screamed for some one to save her
children. Not a man stired, not a man moved.
Yes, one, a poor, hard working carpenter with a
wife and little ones at home, felt his heart beat
and roar with sympathy, and with almost, su-
perhuman strength he forced himself through
the crowd, and in defiance of fire and flame and
smoke, he ascended the ladder rung after rung.
The walls might cave, the fire might burn, the
flames might roar, he was determined to save
those children. When he got to the top he took
them in his arms, and as he was coming down,
he tore his own ragged coat from his body to
shield them from the fire, and placed his own
body between them and the flames. When he
got to the bottom he was dying, and his last
words were, "thank God they are saved." Hun-

dreds of years ago the great tenement house of this world was burning with sin, and every God-loving mother was crying tears of blood for their children to be saved. A poor carpenter by the name of Jesus arose from the waters of the Jordan in the arms of John the Baptist, and ascended the rungs of the ladder of sorrow and took from the very top of the burning tenement house of sin all that would be saved. The fires of hatred burned and blackened and blistered his body with sorrow. Yet he worked on and on, with love and compassion for the salvation of mankind, worked and suffered, suffered and worked. Now as then his arms are ready and willing. Throw yourself on his bosom and he will carry you to a place of safety.

I REMEMBERED GOD AND WAS TROUBLED.

The 77th chapter of the book of Psalms, first six words of third verse: "I remembered God and was troubled."

In the light of the living and the dark of the dying sinner the words of my text are often echoed against the walls of conscience. I remembered God and was troubled. All God-believing people often in the remembrance of God become troubled over their sins; were this not so the church of Christ would be for rent. If you commit a sin and think of God your conscience will surely trouble you, if you have any, and if you haven't got any conscience I surely pity you, for yours is a bad case indeed. Some people get all of their religion from the dining table and carry it in their stomach. I know a man that belongs to the church; when his stomach is full he reminds me of an angel, but when it is empty he reminds me of the Devil. When our religion comes from within instead of without, we are safely anchored on the waters of salvation, but when it requires full stomachs or pleasant surroundings to make us good, we are like feathers in the storm, blown hither and thither, and only stop when the wind stops. Did you ever see a great, overgrown bull dog of a husband come home pitching things here and there, and fussing at everybody and everything. Simply because his sweet, little, troubled-loaded wife didn't have dinner ready just on time; and when dinner was ready did you ever watch the old glutton sit down and eat like an old bear, careless of the comfort and pleasure of others? Well I have, and after his old craving stomach was packed as tight as sardines in a can, his frowns would vanish into smiles, and then the children would begin to laugh and play, even the poor, meek, Christian wife would dare to throw her arms around the old brute's neck and kiss him. The whole house would seem lit up with fearless joy. What a transformation, and all made out of cabbage and pork and turnips. There are just such men in the church and they are always ready to thank God for his bountiful mercies when their old hides are stuffed with the good things of this earth, but when they are hungry they don't think of God or anybody or anything but something to eat. Such people are not Christians, they are heathens; their stomach is their idol and if they have any conscience it can be found in their digestive organs. If such people ever get to Heaven they will have to die with a full stomach, for that is the only time they are ever half way decent. How many of you husbands treat your wives as servants when they are often your equal, and more often your superior. Many of you make beggars of your wives. If they want to spend a little money, or visit a neighbor, you expect them to ask you. When you go home you carry frowns but expect your wife's face to be wreathed in smiles. After you eat your supper your days work is over and you sit brooding over your business troubles, as cross as an old bear, while your wife washes the dishes and puts the children to bed and darns Johnnie's stockings and patches Mary's dress and sews a button on your coat. Then you begin to talk about the work you have to do and how tired you are, never once thinking about the trials and cares and work of your poor wife. Don't you know that your wife has more cares and troubles in one day than you have in a whole week. When Sunday comes you rest and there is a frequent lull in your week days work, but when Sunday comes to your wife there are many things that can not be left undone; the children must be cared for, and you expect to have everything just so. I tell you there is not a man in this town that would swap places with his wife for one week, and yet some of you are always finding fault. I don't care if you have belonged to the church all of your life, you have got a heart of stone. I once received a present from a friend. It came by express in a nice, large box and was labeled in big, black letters, "apples." Now apples was just what I wanted. I was very eager to open that box, and when I got the hatchet and opened the box I found the apples, but they were all rotton. That is just the way with some of you church members. You are labeled with the word Christian in big, flaring letters. You are all right on the outside, but when the box is opened the apples are rotton.

So many people wait for all of the idols of their life to crumble before they remember God, then they are troubled indeed. There are many heathens in this country, both in and out of the church. Mr. Glutton worships his stomach. When he gets dyspepsia so bad he can't eat he'll remember God and be troubled in two ways, then perhaps he'll become a Christian. Mr. Miser worships gold. I can spell his God with the letters of dollar. He says to himself I wear the face of a Christian now, but when I get rich I'll wear the heart of a Christian. Watch out, when you remember God it may be too late.

Miss Vanity worships fine clothes and fine hats and fine jewelry. She thinks more of the treasures of this earth than she does of the treasures of Heaven. Watch out, or you will get up some morning and find that the moths and rust have destroyed all of your Gods, and you will have nothing but the flames of Hell to clothe you. Mr. Fault-finder you are permitted to find fault with your wife and every one else now, but if you do not remember God in time your future fault-finding will have to be with the Devil in Hell. I like fine clothes and fine jewelry and fine carriages and fine houses, and fine everything else, but I like God better. God permits us to use the good things of earth—some of the richest kings were the favorites of God—but to be a Christian God must be first. Abraham loved his son Isaac, loved him perhaps as much as a father ever loved a son, yet he was willing to sacrifice that son to God.

God made the boundless canvas of the universe and pinned every star and sun and moon in its place. God gave to man the breath of life and all that he receives and enjoys belongs to God. We are but beggars in the great poor house of earth. All of our necessities and comforts and luxuries are wheeled to us on the golden chariot of God's mercy. He that loves and worships the things of earth more than God is a traitor to the fountain that quenches his thirst, and surely deserves the wrath of God.

Oh! guilty, sinful man, burn all of your idols in the furnace of the past and remember God and be troubled. Make God first. Let the things of earth be last for the sake of Christ and your own eternal salvation. Throw aside the gold and guild of vanity; do away with the hatred and fault-finding and sham of worldliness. Remember God at the feet of Christ with a heart running over with tears of repentence. Remember God in the name of Jesus, so that you may receive a crown of peace from the New Jerusalem of God's mercy and Christ's love. Yes, a crown of peace on earth and endless joy in Heaven. There is no death for your soul; it must live forever, in Heaven or in Hell. It is but a few steps from the cradle to the grave. Your body will soon crumble back to earth; your love and pride and anger and hatred for things of earth will die with your body; your bonnets and silks and satins and jewelry and carriages and houses will be of no use to your soul. After the night of death is the splendors of Heaven in the day of eternity that will make the soul happy or the horrors of Hell that will make it miserable. Who would give a fortune for a penny, and yet there are thousands of people that would swap eternal happiness for a few moments of worldly

pleasure. There are those that would give
Heaven itself for one night in the ball room;
that would live in Hell forever before they would
bend their proud knees before Christ and beg
God for forgiveness. Poor, weak, vain peacocks
standing on the back of earth, can not you understand that it is the very silken and golden
feathers you wear on your backs that fattens you
for the slaughter house of hell. Oh, sinners, has
the passions of your body so blackened the windows of your soul that the light of God and
Heaven does not shine into your heart? Can
you see nothing but death at the end of life? Do
you see no star of hope beyond the grave? Have
you lost all memory of the cares and sorrows
and teachings and prayers of your poor old sacrificing Christian mother? Is there no power in
her hot tears of sorrow to quench the flames
of your sins? Do you want the earthly part of
your sweet old mother to be eternal? Have you
no desire to hold her hand in the presence of
God on the golden shores of Heaven? Is your
heart hardened against remorse and dead to pity?
Oh, God! I pray Thee open the eyes of every
sinner in this house, draw back the curtains of
the past and show them Jesus standing in the
judgment of Pilate; let them see the hideous
face of the Devil that holds the lash; let them
see the force and fury of the whip with its leaden

pellets of unbearable pain, and as Jesus is
whipped and tortured and fainting let them see
the blood of Christ running from the stripes and
and bruises of the cruel whip and if there is still
no pity in their worldly hardened hearts, show
them the crown of pricking thorns dyed with
blood; carry them to Calvary and let them see
great nails driven by the hand of ferocious
cruelty in the quivering flesh of Christ, and as
Jesus hangs on a cross between earth and
Heaven, bleeding and dying, perhaps their
worldly-hardened hearts will be softened by the
touch of pity, and when Jesus cries in his dying
agony, "Father in thy hands I commend my
spirit," remorse may take possession of their
souls and as they look up into the compassionate
face of our dying Savior they may throw themselves at the foot of the cross and beg for forgiveness.

SERMON.

The revelation of St. John, 20th chapter 15th verse: ''And whosoever was not found written in the book of life was cast into the lake of fire.''

Did you ever go to a great furnace and see ton after ton of metal and rock and coal all fanned to a white heat, and as the melted metal was run off into great ladles ready for the moulds, did you think how horrible it would be to see one of your best friends fall over into so much awful heat? In one moment that friend would be rendered into smoke and ashes. A cry, a shriek and perhaps a few bubbles and all would be over, but oh, the horrors of that one moment, we can only partly imagine. The great despair that would go rushing through the brain of our doomed friend before his body was completely swallowed in the lake of fire. Not even a bone, or tooth or hair would be left to show the awful death. But there is one thing that would be left, and that is the soul—no fire could destroy it. It might burn and squirm and shriek and suffer for thousands of years; the fires might grow hotter and hotter and the agony of every moment might become worse and worse and yet there would be no destruction for the soul; it will live forever. Beyond the darkness of death are the brilliant lights of Heaven or the awful gloom of Hell, and every soul must wing its way to one or the other. Before I became a Christian, I had my doubts about Hell, but that was because I had my doubts about God and Christ and the Holy Bible. I knew if there was a Hell I would surely roast on the grid irons of eternity if I continued on my sinful way and I therefore tried to reason myself up to the belief that the horrors of Hell lived only in the imagination of the fanatic. In studying the Bible I am not led to believe that God created Hell to scare people into Heaven. On the contrary he made Hell to hold the wicked from the good and to punish people for their sins. I can not understand how any man in his right mind that believes in the Bible can doubt the existence of Hell. As sure as there is a Heaven there is a Hell. The words of my text prove it, and every living person out of Christ is standing on the very edge of the great crater of death, and the force of the next moment may push them over into the boiling, burning, hissing volcano of eternal Hell. Parent, if you was standing at the foot of a great mountain and saw your little child

away up on top in its infantile ignorance lean-
ing over the edge of a great hole looking away
down into the very bowels of the earth at a white,
hot lake of melted rock and lead and iron and
dirt, and listening to the awful roar of the min-
eral waves as they dashed with unbridled fury
against the rocky ribs of that burning volcano.
Would you quietly fold your arms and with
tearless eyes and happy heart look away up to
your sweet little darling and smile at its awful
danger. No, mothers, no! No, fathers, no; a
thousand times no! Your whole being would
be changed into breathless, frenzied agony. No
goat ever climbed the Rockles as you would
climb that mountain; there would be no rocks
too large for you to pass; no place too steep for
you to climb. You might be several miles off,
and every mile would seem like a thousand, yet
you would run on and on; thorns might stick
and scratch and tear, rocks might bruise and cut
and as you ran, tired and bleeding, you would
find no time for rest until you had snatched your
darling from the burning jaws of death and carried it to a place of safety. Christians, all of you
have a child or father or mother or sister or
brother or friend that is at this very moment
standing on the dangerous mountain of sin, moving in their blindness around the crater of eternal punishment apparently waiting for the

breath of death to blow them into the fiery lake
of Hell.   All of the ship wrecks and train
wrecks of earth are not one thousandth part as
frightful as one soul wreck.   All of the pains of
every living thing of earth that has lived and do
live and will live, can not be near so great as the
endless pains of a lost soul; for it must suffer
forever and forever.   You can not save your
child, relative or friend, but you can pray and
advise and plead until their sin-hardened hearts
are softened for Chris t to enter and take possession of their souls and help them in safety until
death frees them for Heaven.   There is in India
a cave that is literally alive with squirming,
poisonous reptiles.   No.man has ever entered
that cave to return.   A few years ago a young
Englishman determined to explore it in defiance
of all entreaty of his friends.   One bright morning he, with several others, went nearly to the
mouth of the cave, and as he entered his friends
stood on the outside and looked, and before he
got out of sight the poisonous cobras began to
strike with all of their hissing fury.   He turned
to run, but like a flash of lightning, in a moment's time he was almost completely enveloped
in a living ball of maddened, writhing, hissing
snakes.   He fell and rolled and shrieked in
agony until death brought him relief.   Is there
a person in this house that would dare to enter

that cave? I believe not. And yet, unless your name is written in the book of life, you are going directly towards the lake of fire that burns in eternal Hell, and it is worse than all of the snake bites and deaths of earth. The young man that tried to explore India's snakey cave was governed by his own stubborn will, and it carried him to a horrible death. You that are on the road to Hell are following your own choice. God made the waters and the land and those that care for life do not jump in the water to drown, but prefer to stay on the dry land for safety. If this house was burning down would any of you remain to be bathed in the burning flames of death, or would you get up and out as quick as possible. Oh, sinner, can you not understand that it would be far better for you to have your body burned and blackened and blistered with the fires of earth than to have your soul contorted and charred and twisted with the fires of Hell. If you love life prepare for everlasting life. If you love happiness throw yourself in the arms of Christ and beg God for the eternal happiness of Heaven. If you dislike pain and sorrow, flee from the pain and sorrow of ceaseless Hell. Knock and it shall be opened unto you. Remember that you must first become a lamb of Christ before your name is written in the book of life. The best sinner on earth is

not sheltered with the glorious promise of salvation. When I was a sinner I often said to
myself I am as good as Mr. So and So; he belongs to the church and does many things that I
would not do, and if we both should die I'll get
to Heaven as quick as he will. I feel tonight
that I was right; my chances was as good as his,
but both of us would have gone to Hell. But it
was because neither of us loved Christ. All of
the morality and churches on earth can't save
our souls; it is Christ that does that. What do
you think of a man that would for years and
years do everything in his power to gain your
friendship and confidence and, finally, when he
discovered that you had your pockets full of
money would lure you off to some secluded spot
to rob and murder you? You will undoubtedly
say such a man deserved to be hung—burnt. No
death would be too horrible. Sinner, the Devil
is treating you this way every day in hundreds
of different ways. He pretends to be your friend
and is ever waiting for the seclusion of death to
murder your eternal happiness and rob you of
your soul. As you judge the murderous traitor
to yourself, you judge yourself, for by not trusting in Christ you are a traitor to God, and by
your example you are helping the Devil to murder the eternal happiness of your best friends. I
once saw an old gray-haired, sinful father bend-

ing with tearful eyes over the dying form of a sinful son, and if pity ever took possession of my soul it did when I heard that son say in his dying agony, "Father, you have led me to hell," that poor old gray-haired sinner trembled like a tree in a whirlwind; great tears of unconsolable sorrow ran down his wrinkled cheeks and with one loud shriek of agony he fell fainting on the dying form of his lost son. But let us with a hand of pity draw a curtain over the dying and fainting sinners and quietly enter the loving home of Christian parents and silently listen to the dying words of a Christian child: "Goodby, mama! goodby papa! You taught me right. I am going to Heaven; do not cry, do not sorrow, you will soon meet me there. When you die I will come with Jesus hand in hand and guide you to our eternal home," and as the soul silently leaves the delicate form of that Christian child, we feel that it hovers around its loving parents and gently impresses their hearts with consolation, and as they on bended knees thank God that their darling is saved. We can almost hear the rustling wings of God's angels of mercy as they soar aloft to the heavenly city of eternal joy. Oh, sinner! there is a Heaven and Hell—the Holy Bible speaks of both, and God has implanted in the heart of every heathen an inborn fear of eternal punishment and hope of eternal joy.

There are enough crowns left in Heaven for every person who will live; there is also enough room in Hell to hold the soul of every sinner that will die. Jesus Christ suffered, bled and died on the Cross of Calvary so that you might wear one of Heaven's crowns and if you will shoulder the cross of Christ the crown for you in Heaven will give a refreshing shade of consolation to all of your earthly sorrows, and when the trials and cares of earth find an end in death the ministering angels of God's mercy will guide you beyond the vale of tears, and Jesus, standing on the endless shores of time, with a sweet smile, will crown you with eternal happiness.

SERMON.

Epistles of Paul, the Apostle, to the Romans, 10th Chapter, 13th verse: "For whosoever shall call upon the name of the Lord shall be saved."

The bloodhounds of hell may snap and bark and bite; the cauldrons of damnation may boil and hiss and bubble; demons of crime may laugh and jeer and steal and murder, yet this sacred promise to mankind will stand without alteration until the great end of all that is earthy. This is a broad promise covering every nation and every land. The sin-dyed criminal in his cell awaiting his awful doom at the gallows, feeling and knowing that there is no pity in the laws of man, can take refuge under the roof of this gracious promise; every living thing on earth may desert us, disease may blow his hot, fever-parching breath against us; misfortune may fall like a mighty hailstorm on and around us, still we have the heart-soothing lines of our text from the Creator of all things to comfort us.

Throw the bitter, worm-eaten apple of sin into the silent gulf of the past and call on God through Jesus Christ for rescue. Call on him with tears of penitence gushing from a sin-hardened heart. The Devil may gnash his teeth with malignant defiance and all Hell may persuade and curse and fret and fume, still the gate of salvation will be opened unto you Christ lived and suffered; Christ suffered and died for every sinner's sake; for your sake and for my sake. No star shines as bright as the star of Christ's love. There is no road as smoothe and plain and straight and free from rocks and thorns as the road to Heaven. So many sinners seem to fear the laws of man more than the laws of God; seem to strive for the gathering sham of worldly happiness more than the eternal joy of everlasting Heaven. How often do we hear young Mr. Reckless say, I would shoot that horse if it wasn't for the law. How often do we hear Mr. Money-lover say, I know how to make a fortune in a few months if it wasn't for the penitentiary, or Mr. Murderer say, I'd kill that man if it wasn't for the gallows. It would be far better for you to fear the law of God, the gallows of death and the penitentiary of Hell. There are many that do not commit crime against the laws of the land simply because they fear those laws. Know you that if you foster crime in your heart that it is just as mean in the eyes of God as if you had already committed it.

There are even church members that will give permission to their children to do wrong, and try to persuade themselves that they are Christians. I tell you, you had just as well try to cure hunger by rubbing your stomach on the outside with a beefsteak as to try to get to Heaven by merely being a church member. God gave no one the permission to sanction evil, and those that do are as guilty in the eyes of God as the one that does the evil. Before I was converted it seemed to me that the hardest thing on earth was to be a Christian. Now it seems to me that the hardest thing on earth is to be a sinner. When the snow of sorrow falls there is no roof of comfort to shelter a sinner from the chilly blast; no comfort in prayer; no hope in death. When we are weighed down with misfortune, and the knife of sorrow cuts great bleeding, torturing gashes in our lives if we dare not turn to God, the architect and ruler of all, for relief, where then is comfort? We have many physicians and much drugs for the body, but all frequently fail. For the soul we have but one doctor and he is God. Use the medicine of prayer as he has prescribed it and the words of my text will be fulfilled—you will be saved. You are in a burning building; fire and flame and smoke seems to have cut off every avenue of escape. Suffocating, burning, blistering death

stares you boldly in the face. Oh, how miserable you must be. Brave firemen are working on
the outside and doing all they can to save you.
The fire engine is puffing and blowing and
throwing water, but in defiance of all, your
doom seems sealed. At last you think of death
and God; you fall on your knees and pray as you
never prayed before, and in the very midst of
your prayers the brave firemen snatch you from
the fiery jaws of death. Oh, what a happy moment for you that you feel like a new being.
You have been born again. The sun shines
brighter than it ever did before; the grass is
greener and all nature seems to rejoice with you.
I tell you the home for earthly happiness is in
the household of God. I am a Methodist, but
the Methodist church never saved me; it was the
blood of Jesus Christ that did that. I was a
Christian before I became a church member. I
joined the Methodist church because it is more
agreeable to my views, and I thought gave me a
better chance to do good. However, I am not
working for the Methodist church I am working
for God. My advice is to every sinner, repent
and be saved, then join any church you please.
There is entirely too much wrangle among
church members; there is no time for useless ar-
gument, the great object of all is salvation.
Stick to that object and you will be all right.

Church prejudice is the greatest guilt. Some
church members will have to answer for it in
the final day of judgment, and I tell you if you
don't watch out it will weight your soul down to
Hell. Mrs. Goodbody and r. Neversin belong
to different churches, and they never meet without running down each other's church. Both
imagine themselves awful good Christians. I
tell you I had rather quarrel over the icy corpse
of my dearest friend than quarrel over the religion of Jesus Christ. If you are guilty of ridi-
culing other churches than your own pray to
God for forgiveness and never be guilty of the
same sin again. Give every one the same rights
that you would have yourself. Every Christian
church is a spoke in the wheel of life running
into the great hub of salvation. So let us work
together for each other and for the salvation of
mankind. If our neighbor goes wrong do not
kick him down, but gently and kindly strive to
raise him up. The cruel treatment of the world
ofttimes makes drunkards and criminals of those
that would have been good Christians if some
one had sympathized and prayed with them. A
man goes wrong; society turns him out, and ofttimes the church frowns upon him, and he tries to
drown his sorrow in drink. Drowning sorrow
with whisky reminds me of pouring coal oil on
a dog's back and setting a match to it for killing

fleas. It will kill the fleas every time but it is mighty hard on the dog· Whisky may kill your sorrow for a little while, but it is mighty hard on your constitution and your soul.

If you have any sorrows you want to drown take them to Christ and God will fill your soul with the wine of joy. There are those who will try to push and pull you down the road of sin, but if you will call upon the name of tho Lord, He will save you, and there are hundreds of good Christian men and women that will ever be ready to give you a helping hand along the road to Christ. The good child tries to please its parents; and when it meets with encouragement how its little heart throbs with pleasure. Try to please your Father which is in Heaven and He will give you encouragement in a thousand different ways, and your heart will throb with heavenly pleasure beyond the power of words to express. I speak from experience. The happiest moments of my life are those I devote to God. My sinning friends, on your side of the river of life are mountains and rocks and sand. Everything is dry and parched and burnt. On my side of this self same river are rich and fertile lands covered with luxuriant vegetation. The air is permeated with sweet aroma from most beautiful flowers; sparkling waters, cool shade, sweet berries and luscious fruits are found in every direction; there is a ferryboat built of the timbers of Christianity running from your side to my side, Jesus Christ is the ferryman and the fare is prayer. Pay your fare and Christ will bring you over. When you get over here and look back you will understand by comparison how desolate you were. Don't think for a moment that by becoming a Christian you bury happiness, on the contrary you bury sin and become more happy than ever. I have often heard it said that sin would do to live by, but that it would not do to die by. My sinner friend, you never made a greater mistake in your life. Sin produces nine-tenths of the misery of this life and all of the misery in the life to come. Now is the time. Fathers and mothers, sisters and brothers, uncles and aunts and cousins and neighbors, now is the time to work and pray and plead and cry with and for your sinner relatives and friends that are wandering in blindness out of the fold of Christ. Yes, pray and plead and cry, Hell is near, Heaven is near, life is short, the sword of death is striking hard and fast all over the world and no one knows who will be next. Oh, sinners! if the prayers of your father and the tears of your mother, and the entreaties of your friend, and the love of Christ, and the promise of God all fail to soften your sin-hardened hearts tonight, I will feel like falling on my knees and praying prayers of bleeding anguish for your salvation, until you are either dead or saved. Oh, that you could feel as I feel. Oh, that my heart could send with one mighty throb one drop of my love for our Savior into your sin-hardened hearts and cause them to soften and swell with penitence to Christ. Oh, God! forgive me if this be ambition, it is ambition for Thee and my brothers and sisters through the blood of Adam.

SERMON.

Acts of the Apostles, 27th Chapter, part of the 7th verse: "Saul, Saul, why persecutest thou me?"

There are thousands of good Christian men and women that have heard these very words ringing in the ears of their conscience before they ever thought of falling at the foot of the cross and begging God for mercy. Misfortune after misfortune must weigh the hearts of some people down in sorrow before they will turn their faces towards Heaven and give their hearts to Christ. Sickness must hover around the fireside and even death must take from our homes those we love best before some of us will turn from the Devil and go to Christ for consolation. The sin-dyed thief hanging on the cross by the side of Christ never thought of repentence until torturing pain was trying to open the doors of life so that his soul might go flashing on into eternity. Mother, father, the sunshine of your home has passed away; your darling baby has left the cradle empty; you saw its sweet little waxen body lowered into the cold, damp grave—you went back

home weeping great tears of unconsolable sorrow, and in your home where peace should find
a resting place you could not turn without seeing something that reminded you of the joy that
had fled. A little shoe, a tiny stocking or a
broken doll, all mementoes that would cause
your heart to swell with pain. You had been
following the Devil all of your life; out of the
fold of Christ. Your lips had long since forgot
to frame the infantile prayer your sweet, old
mother taught you. Did the Devil whom you
had followed through all of the years of the past
fill up the great void your innocent prattling
babe had left? Did he whisper words of sympathy that grew into hope and consolation? No,
a hundred times no. He filled your heart with
despair and left you in your misery and there
shedding bitter tears of mental anguish over the
empty oracle of your lost darling, Christ came,
gently knocking at the door of your pain-racked
heart, and you allowed him to enter. Oh, what
a wonderful instantaneous transformation, the
lights of Christ's love blazed into wonderful
brilliancy and lit. up every darkened corner of
your life with consolation and hope. You looked
up, and through the veil of rapidly drying tears
you saw your darling an angel in Heaven, hap-
pier than you and earth could possibly make it
had it been spared to you. Then and there you

renounced the Devil and shouldered the cross of
Christ. Your sweet child's mission was to open
your heart to Christ and then wait in Heaven
for your coming; and oh, what a happy moment
that, when a Christian's soul breaks through its
temple of clay and goes soaring aloft to meet the
loved ones that have gone before. "Saul, Saul,
why persecuteth thou me?" Sinner, sinner,
why persecuteth thou Christ? Paul was cursed
with blindness before his heart was softened to
Christ. Are you waiting for God to take away
your sight and bend your form with grief? Does
it require some great calamity to turn your foot-
steps from the path of sin? Sinner, you are in
the very center of a great calamity. Now your
eyes are covered with the scales of sin; circles of
Hell have blinded you to Christ; you are stumb-
ling in darkness; great ditches of death are before you and behind you, and around you—your
next step may be your last. Christ is here with
the divine ointment of love; he is in every Christian's heart; he is on that bench, and that bench;
he is sitting by your side; he is tugging at the
strings of your heart, but the Devil is on the in-
side holding the latch down. There is a great
fight going on away down in your soul --it is between God and the Devil—which side will you
help? The Devil holds the fort, but he holds it
for ruin—eternal ruin! You have the right to

choose. Your heart is your own. You are free
to make your choice—the Devil offers you
Hell, Christ offers you Heaven. If you let the
Devil hold Christ out of your heart he may
never offer to enter it again. Sinner in your
greatest affliction did you ever think of falling
on your knees and praying to the Devil for relief? Did you ever expect any permanent good
from his advice? You have often sought his
apples of pleasure, and no matter how rosy and
tempting they were on the outside you have always found them rotten and worm-eaten at the
core. You never did a bad thing in your life
that didn't make you feel worse. You never
did a good thing that didn't make you feel better. God rewards you on earth and in Heaven
for your good deeds; the Devil rewards you on
earth and in Hell for your bad deeds. God's
earthly rewards are self respect, a clear conscience and a pure mind, free from the awful
fear of eternal punishment. God's Heavenly
rewards are unmeasurable happiness through all
eternity.

The Devil's earthly rewards are a seared conscience and impure mind racked with discontent
and often drunkenness and prisons and the gallows. The Devil's eternal rewards are Hell and
fire and gnashing of teeth and torturing agony
forever and forever. Christ lightens the burden
of life—the Devil makes them heavier.

The heart of a pure Christian is an eden of joy that lights up the darkened room of sickness and feeds the hungry orphans of poverty. Sinners, the blood of Christ gave you the civilization you now enjoy. It loosened the fetters of slavery from womanhood and made her the purifying essence of home, and turned the heathen brute man into the kind and loving son and husband and father. Our national prosperity is nourished by the blood of Jesus; our moral laws were rolled to us from Calvary on the wheels of many centuries. You that deny Christ would not for all of the world take your family and live among the heathens of Asia. And why not? Because you know your children would grow up in vice. While you are not a Christian you are gathering and enjoying the fruits of Christ's planting every day. You will not water the roots of the tree of Christianity, yet you are unwilling to live without the fruits. You may be bad yourself, but when it comes to your children you would rather see them in Sunday school or church than the saloon or gambling house. Then why persecuteth thou Christ; he was your friend, he is your friend—give your hearts to his keeping. He never did, he never will betray a trust, while the Devil never did and never will fulfill a promise. It is true that great black clouds of sorrow sometimes overshadow a Christian's life but every cloud has a bright lining and the sun of eternal joy shines beyond. If the sky of life was always cloudless there would be no rain to water happiness. Every cloud of a sinner's life grows darker and darker until the grave is reached and then every star of happiness ceases to shine. I once stood on the very top of a snow-capped mountain out in Colorado. I looked down from my lofty height and saw beautiful Manitou nestling at the foot of Pike's Peak; farther on I saw Colorado Springs, and still farther I saw clear, crystal lakes sleeping on the bosom of a great prairie that stretched off to the distant horizon. Every thing seemed green and warm and happy away down hundreds of feet below. Oh, how awful was my loneliness. I was standing on snow rocks and snow and ice surrounded me. Everything was desolate and cold and barren. It seemed to me that I was removed from earth, and there in all of my loneliness I heard the very words of my text ringing away down in my sin–hardened heart, but I heeded them not. I lived on in sin, until every impression of Christ's call faded from my mind. I have thanked God a hundred times since for giving me another chance before it was too late. That other chance came to me down at Waco, Texas. My whole body was hot and burning with fever. For three long weeks I suffered with

intense pain, between life and death. My noble
wife and sweet little baby girl were with me at
the time. Often I was delirious, then I imag-
ined I was in Hell and as my fever grew hotter
and hotter I thought the Devil was pouring red
hot coals of fire all over me. I would twist and
roll and shriek with agony. I would beg for
mercy, but the Devil would laugh at my misery
and heap more coals on my blistered body. My
poor wife sat by my side through the whole of
my sickness, and gave me the medicine the good
old doctor prescribed, and nursed and watched
with aching heart and sleepless eyes. The doctor
advised my wife to rest and sleep, but no, I, her
husband, was on the very brink of death. She
would allow no one to do anything for me. If I
threw the cover off she was there to gently re-
place it. If I groaned she was there to sympa-
thize with me, and not until life gained the vic-
tory over death and I was out of danger could
she be persuaded to rest. Then her whole being
changed—the reaction came. The strain was so
great, my watchful, sleepy, tired wife almost
fell by my side. The sleep she so long needed
came in a death-like slumber. It was a bright
but cold Sunday morning, the room was warm
and comfortable; our little baby girl was laughing and playing on the carpet, and as I laid by
the side of my sleeping wife in my convalesence

and listened to the innocent laughter of my darling baby, I realized for the first time that I was saved for earth, saved for wife, saved for child. Then and there I thanked God from the very bottom of my heart. Then the words of my text that thrilled my being on the top of Pike's Peak once more touched the strings of my soul: "Saul, Saul, why persecuteth thou me." I looked back over the tracks of my past and trembled with emotion. A silent prayer for forgiveness left my heart and winged its way to Heaven. That prayer was answered. God touched my heart with the wand of forgiveness; the scales of sin fell from my eyes. I was almost dazzled with the brilliant lights of joy. Oh, how I thank God I was not only saved for earth and wife and child, I was saved for God and Heaven and eternity. My greatest blessing came from my greatest misery. Christ offered me salvation in my health and solitude on a frozen peak of the Rockies and I refused it. Christ offered me salvation in the presence of my wife and baby, and my sickness prized open my heart for Christ to enter and save me. When I went to Waco I was a sinner, when I left I was a Christian. In my sinful life I cared nothing for my own soul or the souls of men. My business was a lucrative one in my life of sin. I felt sure of a fortune if I would only bridle my extravagant hab-

its, but after my conversion I felt away down in
my soul that I like Paul was called to work for
souls. I studied long and hard over the matter,
and at last decided to work for the Savior that
had done so much for me. I quit my prosperous business and started in my humble way to
work for God, without even knowing how I
would get a living for my little family and self,
but I felt sure that God would provide for us
some how. I have shouldered the cross of Christ
and with the help of God I am determined to
carry it until my eyes are closed in the sleep of
death. Oh, sinners, take my advice; take the
advice of every Christian in this house; listen to
the voice of Christ crying the words of my text
in the ears of your heart. Eternity is at stake.
Although Paul suffered martyrdom for Christ's
sake, all of his pains and aches and sorrows have
long since ceased to exist, For hundreds of
years he has been enjoying the greatest pleasures of Heaven and will continue to enjoy them
forever and ever, but you are not called on to
suffer for Jesus. That day is past. Christianity
will give you more real joy in one hour than a
whole sinful life would. Oh, how wild and awful is the great battle between God and the
Devil raging away down in your soul. The
Devil is trying to pull you down to Hell. For
Christ's sake and your own soul's sake beg God

for mercy. Throw yourself in the arms of Jesus
and he will save you for Heaven and forever.

SERMON.

St. Luke, viii chapter; part of 53rd verse:
"And they laughed Him to scorn."

While the great inventions of mankind laid in
the cradle of infancy, while every pin and every
match and every hoe and every plow was made
entirely by the hand of man without the aid of
the wonderful machinery of the present, while
the tired hands of mothers and wives and sisters
ached and bled over a few yards of homespun
cloth; while goods of commerce were carted over
tedious roads by the aid of horses and mules and
oxen, invention cried, halt! steam will do the
work. Many were weeping because of overwork,
but instead of clapping their hands for joy they
raised their tear-stained faces and laughed the
very idea to scorn. Nevertheless the water
boiled and steam arose and forced the move-
ments of mighty machinery. But still in the
very midst of revolving wheels and shrieking
whistles there were thousands of faithless toilers

jerring and laughing to scorn the wonderful relief
of this mighty invention; and so it has been from
the very beginning of creation. Mankind will
beg for relief, but when it is offered their very
sorrow is often turned to scorn. Jairus fell at
the feet of Christ and begged him to restore
health to his dying daughter. Jesus, always
merciful to those who call on him, unhesitat-
ingly accompanied Jairus to his home, but the
little girl died before he arrived. All hope had
left the members of that household. Trouble
not the master, thy daughter is dead. These were
the words sent out to the sorrowing father, but
Jesus went on; even death did not cause him to
hesitate. Oh, I can see him now, going through
all of that multitude of curiosity hunters, followed by tearful, heart-broken Jairus. I can
see him as he opens the gate and walks through
the yard and up the steps. The young physi-
cian has no medicine case and no fine clothes,
but still he is the Doctor of doctors. Mrs. Jairus
wipe away your tears, the greatest Doctor of
all is coming. Although the darling of your
heart is dead, Jesus will bring her back to life.
Jairus, he is willing to do more for you than
you asked. Love and trust him; but no, in the
very presence of your dead child, you treat this
great Doctor with disrespect in your own house.
You laugh him to scorn. Oh, what a merciful

doctor, instead of turning on you with words of anger and leaving your house for evermore, he kindly orders all to leave the room, and then takes the twelve-year-old maiden by the hand, and with the wonderful medicine of power calls her spirit back to her body. Oh, Jairus! thy little girl is alive and well. Oh, mother! Jesus has brought thy child back to life. How joyful is the moment. But in the midst of so much joy, do you forget to thank Jesus and beg his forgiveness for laughing him to scorn. So many do. There are thousands of sinners all over the land that are laughing Jesus to scorn every day. Sinners, away down in your heart you fear God and hope to be Christians some day. The time was when your mother or your father or your sister or your brother or your child or yourself was very sick. The doctor was called in, but he or she that was sick grew worse and worse. Another doctor was called, but disease seemed determined to win, and at last when death seemed certain; after all earthly hope had fled, you prayed to God for mercy. You even promised that if your prayers were answered that you would ever strive to be a Christian. As the daughter of Jairus was brought back to life your relative or your friend or yourself was brought back to health. Your prayers were answered. Did you fall on your knees and thank

God for his mercy? Did you fulfill your promise? Did you strive to be a Christian? No, you spoke of fate and said that luck was what did the work. You gave God treatment of contempt and have been laughing him to scorn ever since. Every sin you commit is laughter of scorn to the ears of Christ. Yet he is merciful, both willing and ready to heal and to save. In the very presence of scorn he raised the daughter of Jairus from the couch of death. Sinner you are dead. Dead to Christ. Your body is festering in the grave of sin. The most wonderful Doctor Jesus is here. Call on him and every sinning acquaintance you have on earth may laugh him to scorn. Yet he will take you by the hand and raise you up to life eternal. Every time sorrow is crying, prostrated at the feet of God, the hideous face of the Devil is contorted with the Hellish laughter of scorn. You can see it on the street corners and in the saloons and gambling houses and ball rooms. It even sits around the fireside of fashionable society.

Sinners are never satisfied with themselves. They want company. It's awful pain to the Devil to loose one of his flock. Sinners come to Christ—let the Devil pull and push, jeer and laugh—show your strength for Christ's sake and for the sake of your eternal salvation. While the Devil is pulling and pushing and jeering and laughing, every angel in Heaven is singing and rejoicing, and every Christian on earth is willing and ready to help you fight the battle of glory. It is possible that Jairus and his wife and his household were converted to Christ by the resurrection of his darling child. Take the remedy of salvation from the bottle of God's mercy and it is possible that your example will be the means of converting to Christ those who laugh you to scorn the most. While scorn is used by sin-blackened sheep of the Devil to harden the heart of the penitent sinner, love, pity and prayer is used by the blood-washed lambs of Christ. The one wants you for Hell and the other wants you for Heaven. The one offers you the tempting glass of sin, full of drunkenness, disease and misery, the other offers you the white rose of Christ's love, permeated with the perfumes of brotherly love and peace and everlasting joy. Which will you have? The blood of Christ is dripping from the sin-sharpened claws of the Devil, and will drip as long as a single sinner remains on earth. Sins are claws of Hell opening afresh the wounds of Jesus that bled and suffered and died, while nailed to the cross on Calvary; that wore a crown of pricking thorns, and smarted under the sting of the lash in the hand of hatred; that wept over the sins of mankind, and all for the salvation of a sinful world. As long as you remain a sinner you are giving evil for good; you are driving nails of sorrow into the very heart of Christ and laughing to scorn the mercy of your best friend. What would you think of the child that would laugh to scorn the friendly advice of a dying mother? Oh, how horrible; and yet sinner, you are laughing to scorn the friendly advice of a dying savior, who did and is ever ready to do more for you than your mother ever did or could and yet a good mother is one of the noblest gifts of God to mankind. If you have a mother living your conversion will be a balm of relief to her sympathy-aching heart. If you have a mother dead your conversion will be news of joy that will cause even the chords of the harps of Heaven to vibrate with sweeter music to her angelic ears. If you love glory come to Christ and you will have glory eternal. If you love life come to Christ and get life everlasting. Salvation is a basketful of all of the joy-giving fruits of Heaven. Sin is a basketful of all of the tormenting fruits of Hell. Christ offers you one and the Devil offers you the other. Which do you now laugh to scorn? Many of the fruits of sin are beautiful and tempting on the outside, but every peach of the ball room and every apple of the saloon, and every pear of the gambling house and every apricot of vanity is bitter and worm-eaten under the tempting peel. All of the fruits of salvation are free from the bitterness of death. Every peach of charity is full of the sweet juice of happiness. Every apple of Christian love is permeated with refreshing hope, and every pear of forgiveness is full of luscious joy, and every apricot of mercy is ramified with the sweet odor of friendship. The religion of Jesus Christ ennobles our being; it teaches us to shun all that is evil and seek all that is good. Scorn never sits on the lip of Christianity; it is found around the mouth of the Devil, and is used to weaken the weak and shame the foolish. Penitent sinners pray to God for strength to meet the stinging tongue of scorn with words of kindness from the lips of pity. Heap coals of fire on the head of scorn by doing good for evil. Kind treatment in the name of Christ will soon scare the Devil into silence and cause many of the flock of sin to champion the cause of God.

A poor, weak, ragged beggar was invited to dine one Christmas day with a rich philanthropist, and as the beggar took his seat at the table in his rags, the other guests who were butterflies of fashion laughed him to scorn. The host arose and said those who treat the least and poorest of my guests with disrespect, treat me with disrespect also. This dinner is for my friends. And so it is with the world. Christ is the host, and salvation is the Christmas dinner, and every poor, starving sinner on earth is invited to eat of the bread of life, and they that laugh you to scorn are the enemies of Christ and have no right at the table of salvation. You that come to the table of salvation even in your rags of sin, will find protection in the strength of Christ. Although you may be the weakest of the weak and the poorest of the poor, we ride to Heaven in the carriage of right—not might; we go to glory on the chariot of hearts—not dollars. Rich and poor, high and low, strong and weak. the table of salvation is sitting before you loaded with the sweet confections of Christ's love and heavily perfumed with the flowers of God's mercy. All of the breads and cakes and meats and fruits are the best of the best. All is ready and the bell is ringing. There is room for every hungry sinner on earth. For the sake of your hungry hearts, come. For the sake of all that is good and clean and pure, come. Come, so that in the great end of all that is earthly, the Devil of Hell may not laugh your sufferings of eternity to scorn.

SERMON.

Fourteenth chapter of St. John, 15th verse:
"If ye love me keep my commandments."

The sweet aroma of love permeates every
flower of human happiness. The fragrance of
love guides the birds of the air to the nests of
their young and the wild beast of the forest to
the lair of their offspring. It is the hand of love
that rocks the cradle of infantile innocence and
the lullabies of love that closes its eyelids in
peaceful slumber. Love binds up the cuts and
bruises of careless childhood and soothes the
heartaches of reckless youth. It dares to kiss
the rosy cheek of innocent maidenhood and blend
the hearts of man and woman together. It holds
the family around the fireside and is the one
great spring that waters all of the tender plants
of human kindness; with tearful, sleepless eyes
it bends over the form of sickness and in the
budding of health its sympathetic eyes fairly
dance with joy. It is boundless and unmeasurable, endless and eternal. Jesus Christ standing by the side of the Devil on the cold and
frozen mountain peak of hate, looking down on

a sinful world was the very embodiment of
Heaven-scented love. It showed itself over the
news of the death of Lazarus. It showed itself
in blood trickling down the cross on Calvary.
No wonder there are so many grand and noble
women that love Jesus with all of their hearts
and souls. In Christ's time women were kept
very closely; they were not even allowed to learn.
The priesthood tried to keep them as ignorant
as possible. "Let the words of the law be
burned rather than commited to a woman," was
one of the common sayings of the Rabbi. It
was the love of Christ that tore the veil of ignorance from the face of womanhood and made her
the queen of every happy home. The first person to whom the Savior declared himself the
Messiah was a woman, and without her loving,
untiring work for the cause of Christ through all
of the bloody centuries of Christian martyrdom,
the Christian religion would be a thing of the
past. Oh, mothers and wives and sisters. God
gave you almost unlimited power over the hearts
of mankind. Use it in Christ's name and for
Christ's sake. Mothers commence at the cradle;
wives commence at the altar; sisters commence
at the first false step. And I tell you it will not
be long before every home will be full of the
sweetest flowers of Christian love, and when one
of the chairs of your fireside is made empty by

the icy chill of death, you will know your loved one loved Jesus and obeyed his commandments, and that at the end of life the whole family circle will assemble in Heaven around the fireside of God. The one bitter drop in the sweet cup of a Christian's life is to feel that I am saved and mine are lost. ♦Streams of tears have been shed over the sins of wayward sons and brothers and fathers and husbands, and every tear was sparkling with love.

You passive church members do not love Christ, for you do not obey his commandments. Instead of shouldering the cross of Christ and following him you lay it aside and find a good, soft cushion and there you sit with folded arms in peaceful anticipation of a better world, caring little or nothing for the souls of others. Is that the way to love your neighbor as yourself? Is that the way to confess Christ before men? You passive, comatose church members crawl into the silken cocoon of your conversion and expect to be metamorphosed into Heavenly butterflies. You are not obeying the commandments of Jesus; you are not multiplying the talents of your master, but you bury those that he gives you and can only offer to the Lord that which is already his. You careless, promise-breaking mothers do not love Jesus for you do not keep his commandments. How often in the day do you tell little Johnnie or Mary that you will whip them if they don't do this or stop doing that, and they keep right on doing or not doing and you keep on threatening but you don't whip. You do not only lie to your children, but they soon learn to know it. "Now Johnnie," says Mrs. Busybody, "run out in the yard and get me some chips and I'll give you something pretty." Little, innocent, trusting Johnnie takes the basket and gets the chips and comes back with his great big eyes fairly dancing in hopeful anticipation of his mother's promise. "Now ma, here are the chips. I want my pretty." I havn't got it now Johnnie, but I'll give it to you some other time; but the some other time never comes, and the innocent Johnnie soon learns that his mother is a liar. Oh, what an example to innocent childhood. Suppose all of the promises of God were like the promises of the careless parent, how cold and barren and gloomy would be the future. Every parent should strive to be the same example to the child as Christ was to us—do not drive but lead into goodness. There is more strength in example and persuasion than there is in driving and forcing. Oh, noble Christian mothers, as you love your children Christ loves you, and even much more. All of the comforts of your home are for your children, and all of the comforts of Christ's home

are for you and your children and their children
if you will only love Jesus and obey his commandments. You that think more of your children's bodily comfort than you do of their souls,
must be blind indeed, for what are the comforts
of earth in the scales of eternity—they would not
have the weight of a feather against the weight
of every sun and star and moon of the universe.
Let your efforts for Jesus be untiring and undying through the whole of your life, so the talents
that God gave you may be doubled. If you
would at the end of life hear the glorious words
of "Well done thou good and faithful servant."
Every soul, you as an instrument in the hands
of God, bring to Christ will be a brilliant gem in
your Heavenly crown. You are not called to do
what Peter and Paul and James and all of the
martyrs of the Christian religion have done. It
was their privation and want and stripes and
imprisonment and death that gave us the religion
of Jesus Christ; it was floated to us on rivers of
blood, and is now the most prominent fact of all
civilization.

If James, the brother of Jesus, was stoned for
the sake of Christ, could not you mothers and
fathers devote a little more of your time for the
sake of Jesus and your children..

If Peter suffered the horrors of crucifixion for
Christ's sake and all that have lived, and you,

that do live, and all that will live, could you not work a little more for God? If Paul was stoned and left for dead and was afterwards revived and in defiance of all persecution continued to preach, both to Jews and Greeks, can you not make a few sacrifices for Christ's sake. Think of all of the Christian pioneers in the wilderness of idolatry. Oh, how they cut and dug and grubbed and worked and suffered and died for Christ's sake. Many of them were personally acquainted with Christ in the flesh, and that they believed in Him and suffered and bled and died for him is sufficient proof of the glorious truths of Christianity, had we no other proof. Atheists and infidels are bound to acknowledge Christ every time they date a letter, as all documents of civilization are dated from the birth of Christ. There is no miracle in the Bible so far beyond my understanding as the miracle of disobedience among believers. That you should believe in the glorious rewards of Heaven and the awful punishments of Hell; in the unbounded love of God and the endless hatred of the Devil, knowing that Christ never did a thing that was not for your good, and that the Devil never did a thing that was not for your sorrow. Still you prefer the Devil to Christ. Sinner do you love your good old father? Yes. And why? Because he is your father and has struggled and toiled and

sacrificed so much for you. Why not love God?
He is the father of your father and my father and
everything that was and is and will be. He
gave his only begotten son to the slaughterhouse
of sin so that you and yours and I and mine
might be saved. If the blood of Christ and all
of the hundreds and thousands of Christian martyrs that gave up home and wealth and friends
and life have no power to swell your hearts with
penitence, then yours is a heart of flint. If you
have the heart of a human look and beg for
mercy. Look down, down into the fathomless
eternity; hear the souls of the lost sizzing and
frying on the grid irons of Hell; hear the gnashing of teeth and painful shrieks, amid the nox-
ious fumes of brimstone boiling and bubbling in
the cauldrons of eternal damnation. Hundreds
of thousands of crawling, squirming, burning,
blistered souls, and not a single one loved Jesus
or obeyed his commandments. Look up through
the star-lit sky into the golden streets of perpetual Heaven and there see the divine face of God
wearing the everlasting smile of love, and in the
midst of Heavenly flowers and divine music, see
Paul and Peter and James, and all that loved
Jesus and obeyed his commandments. Over
there in the very midst of Heavenly wonders see
your good old mother and father and sweet little
sister and brother and all of your good Christian

friends. Hold! There is a vacant Heavenly cushion. Sinner, will you take it? Jesus is here tonight willing and ready to write your name on the book of eternal salvation. For the sake of everything that is noble and pure and good, fall before Christ, and with a heart bursting with penitence, give him your name now and forever.

www.ingramcontent.com/pod-product-compliance
Lightning Source LLC
Chambersburg PA
CBHW032019010726
47493CB00007B/2474